PLAYGROUND GAMES

PLAYGROUND GAMES

Ten Short Stories

by

Rev W D R Smith

ASPECT

Playground Games
Rev WDR Smith

Designed, printed and published by Aspect Design
89 Newtown Road, Malvern, Worcs. WR14 1PD United Kingdom
Tel: 01684 561567 • E-mail: allan@aspect-design.net
Website: www.aspect-design.net

A copy of this book has been deposited with the British Library Board

ISBN 978-1-912078-46-2

Contents

TRAIL MIX

Chapter 1

Alan Ledbury looked towards the window as the last rays of the winter sun penetrated into the classroom at the end of a Friday afternoon in February. His pupils sat at their desks writing the exercise that he had set them some three-quarters of an hour previously. In the relative silence he had time to think. What was the real purpose of his life at this present moment? What were his expectations for the future? Would he resign himself to his teaching career until retirement loomed on the horizon? And what then? Soon it would be time to finish for the day, dismiss this last class, gather his things together and drive home. But in these fleeting minutes he had time to think of a possible answer.

It was almost the first anniversary of his wife's death on 19th February. On that fateful day Ann had finally succumbed to the cancer that had invaded her body over the relatively short period of a year. The decline had been rapid towards the last months. Also distressing and destructive of family life, which seemed to have been reduced to a series of medical appointments, hospital visits and radiotherapy. The initial high hopes of a cure faded gradually into painful resignation of the inevitable outcome. The final week of visiting in the hospice had been a harrowing time for him and for Ann. His teenage son Chris had not wanted to accompany him for the last days even though he had been close to his mother.

The funeral was a small affair, the number of those attending being limited to the capacity of the small chapel at the crematorium. Twenty-five minutes seemed a poor allocation of time to evaluate a human life. The subsequent wake was held in the family house, a three-bedroomed terrace of Victorian vintage on the edge of the town. After an hour or so the various relatives and friends once more expressed their condolences and took their leave. It was now the hour of the 'Friday Rush' and everyone would be keen to start for home as the darkness fell. Nothing remained for Alan and his son but to tidy up and put the extra chairs back into their rightful rooms and sit down together in front of the television. By ten o'clock they decided that they might as well go to bed and they both retired to their bedrooms.

Alan woke late the following morning. It was a Saturday and his body had become accustomed to the idea of a lie-in at the weekend, the more so since the time that Ann had not been in the house. Slowly he turned over the events of the previous day in his mind, the funeral, the guests, and the perfunctory attempt at closure. Why was it that crematorium services always seemed to be held on Friday afternoons just when the traffic was at its worst? That was his experience at least.

He made his way downstairs to make some breakfast. His son, a typical teenager not there yet. Teenagers at weekends rarely surface before the afternoon, he thought.

Midday came and went and at one o'clock Alan decided that it was now about time to tell Chris that the day was fast slipping away and so he went upstairs and knocked on Chris' door. No answer. So he called out "It's gone one o'clock. Are you going to town today?" Again, no answer. He opened the door quietly and entered the room. Peering through the darkness occasioned by the drawn curtains he looked around. His eyes focused on the bed. Chris was not in it. Moreover, he was not in the room.

Chapter 2

Alan made his way downstairs turning over the only possible explanations in his mind. Chris had gone to his room at ten o'clock, last night. Alan had seen him enter the bedroom. Where was he? Had he gone out early this morning before Alan got up? Had he left the house during the night? To look at a teenager's bed would not have yielded any clues. It always would look the same, made or unmade, unmade being the default condition. He decided to go into town for an hour and look around the various teenage haunts. Donning his coat he left the house and walked through the estate until he reached the town shopping precinct. It was here that young people tended to gather on benches mid to late afternoon on a Saturday. Several were around, talking loudly and wearing olive green parkas with fur around the hood but Chris was not among them. Alan walked on to a café that the teens frequented, looked through the street window at the clientele, his eyes searching for his son but after a minute or two he moved on, lest he might be considered to be a pervert.

It was five o'clock when he arrived back home. "Would Chris be there now?" he wondered. He opened the door, went in and called. No answer. A quick tour of the house confirmed the fact that he was alone in the house. He decided to wait and sat down in front of the television, hoping that on this particular Saturday the choice of programmes might be more interesting than usual.

By early evening he had grown more agitated and panic was beginning to set in. He had lost his wife and now his son. He tried to recall the close friends that his son had. Only two boys of the same age were really known to him and both had been several times to the house. He decided to phone them up to see if Chris had been with them. Frustratingly the phone calls gave no lead. Both boys had not seen Chris since Friday at school and so he rang the police and reported a missing person.

Chapter 3

It was almost a year now since Chris had gone missing. The school bell sent a shrill sound from the corridor into the classroom. Alan dismissed his class, tidied his desk, gathered the inevitable books to be marked together, packed his briefcase and made his way to the staff cloakroom to retrieve his coat. Without going into the staff room he walked out to the car park, got into his second hand car, a blue Ford Escort and drove home. It was the beginning of the half-term holiday.

Alan had not given up the hope of finding Chris. As he drove home he thought back to the holidays and weekends over the past year when he had visited various locations in the hope of uncovering his son's whereabouts. In twelve months he had toured Scotland, Wales, the North, London, the South-East, the Midlands and the West Country, in fact all the places where they had been as a family. Nowhere was there any trace of his missing son. It never occurred to him that he might never find him. 'Where there's life, there's hope' he mused. But was there life?

He stopped at a garage on the way and filled up with petrol, checked the oil and the tyres, paid and drove home. Now the car was ready for another search mission. But where? He spent the evening cooking a meal and watching television. Eventually after the ten o'clock news he turned the set off and just sat back in his armchair in silence. After a while he walked over to a bookcase where he stored photographs of years gone by and pulled out an armful of albums. Flicking through the first few in a short space of time he then turned to one that bore the inscription "Family Holidays 1968-1970". Memories began to surface as he looked at photos of Ann, Chris and himself and the various locations where they had spent time at Easter and summer during these years. There were coastal views of Scotland, Devon and Cornwall, walks on the Shropshire Hills, cities and historic buildings, camping in Wales and almost four whole pages of the Forest of Dean in Gloucestershire. As he looked at these last pages he noticed that they seemed to have been looked at and used more than the others in the album. An embryonic thought began to arise in his mind. "Could this be a clue to his son's whereabouts? Should he go and investigate?" It was now approaching midnight and any action would have to wait until morning. And so he got himself to bed with the resolve to make a plan of action the following day.

Chapter 4

On Saturday morning Alan ate a hurried breakfast, packed a bag with enough clothes for a few days, made some sandwiches and put all these into the boot of the car. Then he gathered together all the maps he could find of the area in question, a couple of Ordnance Survey maps, a Forestry Commission Forest of Dean walking guide of the forest trails and a road map of Britain and placed these in the front where he could access them more easily. Then he started the engine, drove out of his estate and headed for the motorway, first the M5 and then the M50 to reach the area as quickly as possible.

Within an hour or so he had parked in the Forestry Commission car park at Symonds Yat and was seated on a bench outside the log cabin that served as an information centre and snack bar, drinking a welcome brew of instant coffee out of a plastic cup.

As he drank the coffee his mind went back to family outings and walks along the forest trails, to The Biblins with the footbridge over the River Wye, the ferry down below him, Cannop Ponds and Edge End. He finished his coffee and walked to the viewpoint where one could see the bend in the river and the canopy of the forest. Was this the place where his son had come to? If so, where was he?

He decided to do some exercise for his own good rather than to start haring around looking everywhere since he knew that this would not produce results. He walked down the steep path to the ferry. He knew a circular walk they had done together as a family that took in both sides of the river. After a sharp descent he reached the ferry, hailed it and paid the fare, walked past the Saracens Head public house on the other bank and walked along as far as the footbridge at the Biblins where he stopped for half an hour to eat the sandwiches that he had brought from home. Then he crossed the footbridge and took the path on the other side back to Symonds Yat. As he walked his memory played back the times the family had spent in these woods. Each visit they had selected a forest trail and explored the points of interest. There were mines, or rather had been, now only a few remaining in use, worked by the "Freeminers". There were also places where ordnance had been stored in World War Two and the Speech House where the Verderers had their meetings. He remembered how the family set off on each occasion with a haversack containing food, drink and a map. About half way around each trail they would stop at a clearing or where the Forestry Commission had provided a picnic area and take a refreshment break. Alan enjoyed the challenge of finding the way, Ann the peace and quiet of nature all around, and Chris...what was it that he had liked about the place?

Some hours after he had set off Alan climbed back up the steep slope to the Yat Rock car park and got into his car. The walk had at least dispelled some of his nervous energy and he felt better for it. He would now drive to another part of the forest. He started off but after a few miles there seemed to be something wrong with the Escort's engine. It was not firing correctly and so he stopped. He got out and opened the bonnet and looked inside. There was nothing that he could ascertain as the cause of the fault. He got back in and drove on. The fault persisted and so he stopped again. What to do in such a sparsely populated area? After a wait of a few minutes he noticed a man and a dog walking towards his parked car. As they drew nearer Alan got out. "Good afternoon" said the man. Alan reciprocated similarly and then continued, "I've got some engine trouble. Do you happen to know of anywhere I might get some assistance?" "That's where you're in luck" the man replied "There's a garage about a mile away on the main road." Alan expressed his gratitude and headed off, the engine misfiring all the way. He found the garage, parked, located the owner and explained the problem. Evidently it was a straightforward repair and would take about an hour. The owner suggested Alan could go for a walk or wait in the garage in the meantime. Alan had done enough walking for one day and so he chose the latter. His curiosity caused him to watch the garage owner as he worked on the car. He struck up a conversation. "Do you work here on your own? No apprentice?" The owner explained that he preferred to work on his own and there wasn't a lot of work, just enough to make ends meet. Alan continued with a question more for his own benefit rather than for the sake of conversation and asked "What work would a young lad about to leave school do around here, then?" "Well, the only work around here would be on the land, on the farms. They take school leavers occasionally." was the answer. Satisfied with this response Alan sat down on a bench and waited until the repair was finished. Then he paid the bill, thanked the garage owner and drove off in search of a B and B.

The garage owner had mentioned several B and Bs in the proximity and on the first attempt Alan secured a single room for two nights at a house in the middle of that part of the forest. As the establishment did not provide anything other than breakfast he went out in the early evening and found a local pub serving a limited choice of food. He chose cottage pie with vegetables and sat down in the lounge with a pint of mild ale. After he had finished his meal and ale he went to the bar and got himself a refill. As the barman was not otherwise occupied he ventured to ask, "Do you know how many farms there are around here?" "That depends on how wide an area you mean. It could be anything from half a dozen upwards" was the answer. For the purposes of Alan's task this was sufficient information. He sat down again and when he had finished his drink he returned to the B and B and retired to his room to sleep.

Chapter 5

Breakfast the next morning did in no way disappoint. A pot of tea, cereal, freshly cooked bacon and eggs together with beans and fried bread and toast, butter and marmalade to follow. No wonder that the great English breakfast was hailed as the best thing in English cuisine. Even visitors from abroad agreed on this.

Thus fed and fortified he got his things together, checked his map and went to the car to begin his day's business. The Escort started first time and the engine purred sweetly. The garage owner had done a good job yesterday. He drove to one of the farms made on a list he had compiled from studying his OS maps. The first two farms yielded no result. One seemed to have nobody about and the other had only a farmer and adult son working there. Unsurprised he drove to locate the others. He arrived at one that was at the end of a track, parked the car and got out to see if anyone was about. As he neared the outbuildings he met the farmer and briefly stated his purpose. No, the farmer didn't employ anyone except family. The farm was not large and they could manage. Alan expressed his thanks and drove on. At the next farm he came to he could see that this one had a dairy herd. He parked and made his way towards the large sheds in the yard. He noticed a group of farm workers and among then a distinct figure of a person in their teens wearing overalls, wellington boots and a woolen hat.

He made his way towards the group. The figures turned around as he neared and the one who was clearly the farmer spoke to Alan and asked his business. The farmer introduced himself and the others in the workforce, two adult male farm workers and his teenage daughter who was helping on the farm in her school holiday. Alan had drawn another blank. As he turned to leave he asked "Are there any farms near here that sometimes take on casual workers?" The answer was that there was one at the extremity of the forest that had done so in the past. The farmer provided directions. Wearily, Alan returned to his car and set off once more with very little hope in his heart. After a few miles he located the farm. It looked quite small and less well kept than the others he had visited. It was a dairy farm. He could hear the cattle as he stepped out of the car. He made his way through the farmyard gate and headed for the outbuildings. It was here that he met the farmer. He explained the reason for calling and asked if the farmer had any employees other than himself. The farmer's reply was "Well there is Rob Clarke. He's in the shed. I can take you to him if you like." As they approached the shed he could see a figure forking fodder into the racks. He called out a greeting and the figure turned to look. Alan was looking directly into the face of his son, Chris.

Chapter 6

It was an unusual reunion some half an hour later as they sat around a pot of tea in the farmhouse kitchen – Alan, Chris, the farmer and his wife. Chris explained that his mother's funeral had made him feel constricted with no real outlet for emotions. He also felt that life at school would be difficult at first but then he would have to put everything behind him and knuckle down to work and there would be no time for other thoughts.

Life in his home town would also not help the grieving process. Everyone busy with their own lives and occupations. He needed a break. More than just a few days, even weeks. He wrestled with thoughts of how to achieve this. Eventually a solution began to form in his mind. He would go somewhere to a place he already knew and appreciated. Somewhere remote, not well known, where he could vanish for a while. If he tried to explain this to anyone, friends, relatives, even his father then the whole concept would die a death and life would inevitably continue in a way that he did not think he would be able to bear.

He had left home in the early hours of that Saturday morning after his mother's funeral a year ago, taking only his coat and had walked some miles until daylight. Then by hitching lifts along the way he had arrived at his intended destination here in the forest. At the end of the day he stumbled upon this farm, told his story to the farmer and his wife under the name of Rob Clarke, was taken in by them and as it was now getting dark was given a bed for the night.

The following day the farmer and his wife attempted to persuade him to get in touch with his family but he had refused and wished it to remain so. After the weekend the farmer and his wife had made the decision to respect his wishes and allow him to contact his father or not according to his conscience. They found work for him and gave him bed and board. For a year he had worked for them and apart from evening and weekend walks in the close proximity of the farm he had not ventured any further afield.

Alan was at great pains not to ask the burning question "But why did you not think to tell anyone where you were?" but instead he managed to enquire, "What are your plans now, Chris?" After a short pause his son replied, " Well, Dad, I have found that an open air life suits me and this sort of life would help me to go into the future." Alan asked "So you want to make a career in farming?" Chris responded. "No, not in farming. This year has been a kind of transition. I said I preferred an outdoor life. It is for this reason that I have decided to go into the army. I shall be old enough soon. I shall finish working here and then come home before I go away. That is, if you will have me back." "Of course I will," Alan replied, "and I'm glad I found you alive and well." With this last statement everyone in the room smiled. The forest had given up its secret.

The End

POSTGRADUATE STUDIES

Chapter 1

James White was driving back from work on a warm day in May after an ordinary day in the office where he was employed as a clerk. Two years had now elapsed since he had completed his studies at Birmingham University and he was now living in a rented house in the Midlands. He had spent three years studying English and in the first year of his course he had met Ann, a fellow student studying History and they had spent most of the three years together in a relationship. They had spent their weekends and free time together in the city parks such as Cannon Hill, on the Lickey Hills on the edge of the Black Country and the Clent Hills with their views over the surrounding countryside. James had kept a car while at the university and they had also visited places of mutual interest – locations rich in English history – Iron Bridge in Shropshire, Warwick Castle, Stratford upon Avon and so on. They had enjoyed being together. After their final exams they had become engaged to be married.

Then within the next six months James had begun to have second thoughts, if indeed he had managed to have any serious thoughts at all as he had not settled on a decision about life after university. Unlike other former students, including Ann, James had made no attempts at considering a career or looking for a job. He had stayed at his parents' home spending his time doing nothing or reading books. Eventually his lack of pursuing the idea of a career got on the family's nerves. When was he going to get a job? What about his engagement? Was he just going to sit around for the rest of his life? It was as if the impact and result of three years of concentrated study had drained him of all energy and inclination. He felt 'flat' and mentally exhausted, not wanting to put his mind to anything. Ann wrote letters to him twice a week but he only managed a reply now and then. When she suggested coming to see him he made excuses. In any case they both lived hundreds of miles away from each other, at opposite ends of the country. After some time Ann wrote to say she was ending the engagement. He didn't even reply to her. Despite all his education and time at university he felt empty and disillusioned. Life at the family home had become difficult due to his parents' disapproval and frustration at his inactivity. He decided to move out. Somehow he summoned enough energy to get a job in the office of a factory some twenty miles from home. Soon after he started work and had some money in the bank he was able to find a small house for rent in a village near his place of work and he moved out of his parents' home. What the family thought of this he was not sure but he believed that they considered it a relief and some kind of step in the right direction.

Chapter 2

Some weeks later after work he arrived at his rented house, parked the car on the drive, went in and began to prepare an evening meal, much along the lines of the limited range of student cooking. He had been fortunate to find this small two-bedroomed semi-detached house. He was able to live an uncomplicated and undemanding existence away from home. The village in which the house was situated was quite large and boasted a row of shops, three public houses, a church, a playing field and a hall.

Once or twice a week James frequented The Anchor, one of the pubs where the regulars were mostly locals and there was a Thursday night quiz. His presence at the quiz nights came to be appreciated due to his more than adequate knowledge of both English and History. He was particularly an asset to a team in the spelling round and became much sought after when teams were being formed. Mary, a woman in her early twenties and one of the regulars noticed his ability and contrived to get into his team whenever she could. Mary had set out to discover more about James and one evening after the quiz she sat down next to him and struck up a conversation. She asked about his job and upon discovering that he did quite basic office work she asked about how he seemed to have acquired such a broad range of knowledge. On this occasion James gave nothing away.

In the weeks that followed, Mary was there each evening that James visited The Anchor and on one evening she asked him if he would like to go with her to the cinema one evening in the following week. After some thought James agreed. Perhaps this was a glimmer of evidence that his life was about to turn a corner. Mary established where he lived and said she would call for him in her car.

The film they saw was one that was currently being screened in the provinces after its London première and though sufficiently entertaining it did not hold any great interest for James. Some halfway through the performance James became aware of Mary's body now closer to his and then a hand was placed on his knee. He reciprocated by lightly holding Mary's hand. As they left the cinema Mary invited him to come back to her house for a late night drink. He agreed. Mary's house was a small terraced cottage in the centre of the village. She lived alone. The front door was on the street and on entering they were in the living room that led through to a small kitchen. "Coffee or something stronger?" Mary asked. "What's the 'something stronger'?" James enquired. "I've got Scotch, Gin, Vodka or wine" came the answer. "Well, a small Scotch then." James replied. "That makes two of us" was Mary's answer. They sat down on the large sofa that occupied most of the room, drank their Scotch and talked. Mary persisted with her questions about James' broad range of knowledge that he had displayed during the pub quiz evenings. Seeing no real harm in an answer James told her that he had studied English for three years at Birmingham and had obtained his degree two years ago. Mary seemed both satisfied and impressed with this answer. So much so that she snuggled up to James and kissed him first on the cheek and then full on the lips. This female bodily contact had an arousing effect on James and he returned the kiss. Their bodies began to explore each other's legs, thighs, waists, backs and chests, continuing for some minutes until James drew himself back and said "I really think I must be going now. It's getting late and I have an early start tomorrow." Mary asked coyly "Don't you like me?" "I do", James began "But I really must be going now." With that he took his leave and walked back to his house.

As he got ready for bed he began to ask himself what had happened this evening. Was he ready for this? Was he ready for a new relationship after a space of two years? With these questions buzzing around in his head he tried to sleep. Eventually he succeeded.

Chapter 3

Over the next week he met up with Mary several times, both at the pub and also at her house. He enjoyed having female company as he had done with Ann while studying at university. Whereas Ann had been interested in visits to places of historic interest, castles, great houses and walking, Mary had no inclination for any of these things. She just seemed to be content with sitting in a pub with a drink or at home. Different though this was for James it had been a welcome change in his life.

The physical side of the relationship had grown, too. They had moved on from the sofa to the bedroom albeit at weekends when there was no early start for work on the following day. Then, one evening when James turned up at Mary's he noticed another car parked outside the house. He rang the doorbell and Mary opened the door. As he entered the lounge he came face to face with another man. Recognition was instant. Before Mary came out with the introduction "James, I would like you to meet Tony." James had recognised a former fellow student from their days at university.

James didn't stay more than a few minutes. He left making excuses that he had only called to see if Mary would be at the pub quiz on Thursday, also saying that he wasn't feeling too well and needed an early night. All the same, he was somewhat disturbed by meeting a former fellow student from his university days. Tony had studied physics and was one year below James and Ann. He had been active in the Students' Union and the debating society and was a regular in the students' common room and bar. James had not known him well but they had talked together and Tony had met Ann when she was with James. What was he to do now?

James spent the next few days considering all this. He did not call on Mary again and kept his excuse of not feeling well in reserve in case he was asked why he had not been around. Then on Thursday he made his way to The Anchor. The regulars were milling around with drinks and sorting themselves into teams for the quiz. He looked around the bar. Then he caught sight of Mary in a corner. She was with Tony. James didn't stay. He went back to his house.

It was on Saturday morning at the weekend that Mary called at James' house. At the sound of the doorbell James opened the door and there she was. He also noticed Tony's car outside with Tony sitting in it. "Hello James" she began "Tony and I are just going into town for a pub lunch. Would you like to come along?" James declined the invitation.

When they had gone he went over the situation in his mind. So Mary was not really interested in a steady relationship. If she had turned from him to Tony in a matter of weeks then how long did she give a relationship anyway? Even if he were glad of the company of others he didn't feel like socialising with her and Tony because sooner or later Tony would start talking about the years at university, if he hadn't already, and somehow or other Ann would be mentioned in the course of conversation. James did not relish the idea of this. So he decided to stop seeing Mary and also to stop frequenting The Anchor. He could exist without quizzes. He would however, miss female company.

Chapter 4

As the weeks went by James considered what other interests might be a possibility for the evenings and weekends. Looking through the village magazine he noticed that there was a village choir that met on Monday evenings and the article in the magazine stated "New members welcome". At secondary school James had been in the school choir and had sung tenor. Choirs usually have enough bass voices but tenors tend to be in short supply. It might be possible to find an outlet for his interest here. Accordingly on the following Monday evening he made his way to the village hall at the time advertised and found the room in which the choir met.

The first evening with the choir went well. As expected the tenor section was less well represented and James was accepted as a welcome addition. The songs were varied and he coped well with all the notes. After a couple of hours the practice was over. Details were given about a forthcoming village concert in a few months' time and this gave him some encouragement for the future.

Daily routine continued for James. He went to work Mondays to Fridays but he had stopped going to The Anchor and his only activity was now the Monday choir practice. After the disappointment of finishing with Mary he felt that he needed something else to occupy his time. What could he do? Was there anything he had enjoyed that he wasn't doing now? His thoughts went back to his years with Ann and how they had spent time together. They had enjoyed long walks over the hills and had visited places of historical interest. This was something he missed. To retrieve some of this might perhaps be a way forward. And so, after a few weeks, on a Saturday morning he drove back to one of the locations they had often visited - the Clent Hills.

James parked his car in the Walton Hill Car Park, changed his shoes for walking boots, put on his parka and slung a small haversack over his shoulder. He set off to climb up to the ridge of Walton Hill. He had in mind to walk a circular route that he knew well, over Walton Hill and back via the Four Stones on Clent Hill. Once on the ridge he had a superb view of the surrounding countryside. As he walked towards the village of Clent he remembered the many times that he and Ann had walked these hills in their university days. The hills were quite near to Birmingham and his owning a car while at university had been a real asset, not having to rely on public transport. Besides which he and Ann had preferred to explore the countryside rather than the delights of the city. He thought about their relationship that had a stabilising effect on their studies and which at the time had appeared to have a promising future. But that was now all in the past and he was trying to make some headway into that which might become his life at the present moment. All too soon he was descending the hill and heading across a field to a footpath that led past the church in Clent. He walked past the church, turned right along Odnall Lane and continued till he arrived at The Fountain, a pub below Adam's Hill, that he and Ann had often frequented for a welcome drink and a rest on this route that they had so often taken only a few years ago. On reaching the pub he went in, ordered a pint and sat down to enjoy his drink and rest before the next stage of his walk which would be uphill for quite a long way. After a few minutes he became aware of a woman who appeared to be looking at him. At first he took little notice. Then the woman got up, came over to where he was sitting and said "Excuse me, but aren't you James White who was at Birmingham University a few years ago?" James was momentarily stunned by this question but then he replied, "Yes, I am. Should I know you?" The woman answered, "My name is Sue Brooks. I was a year below you. I studied history." James could not remember having ever met Sue, even though Ann had studied history as well. Sue asked if she could sit down next to him and they began to engage in conversation. As they talked he found out that Sue had not lived in student accommodation as she lived in Hagley, only some 10 miles away and she had commuted daily. In any case, the History Department was quite big and James had only known one historian -Ann – and they had spent most of their free time together.

Sue did know who Ann was and because of this she knew that Ann and James had been an item. That was all. They continued in conversation about what they had both done since leaving university. James had little to tell but Sue had found work as an executive with a local authority in the West Midlands area. After some half an hour James declared that he ought to be getting on with his walk. "Have you visited the church here yet?" Sue asked him. "It's said to be worth a visit." James said that he had passed it on his way to The Fountain but had not gone inside. "Would you like to have a look at it with me?" Sue asked. James' first reaction was to decline the invitation but he reasoned that as he had no concrete plans for the day and the whole idea was for him to explore new possibilities, he decided to accept.

They left the pub, retracing the route by which James had come until they reached the church. They went through the gate, passing the war memorial and entered the building. St. Leonard's, Clent had its origins in the twelfth century. It was built of dark red sandstone. The kings of Mercia had resided at this location and the larger parish was in the early ninth century the scene of the murder of Kenelm, the young son of Kenwulf, King of Mercia, mentioned by Chaucer in the Nun's Priest's Tale in the book of the Canterbury Tales.

Sue's interest in history and James' knowledge of English literature enhanced the visit. They had found a subject of mutual interest. James felt his old study skills and thirst for knowledge slowly awakening. The former feeling of being 'flat' and his inactive state of mind was beginning to dissipate. This mental development, together with being in intelligent female company acted as a catalyst, transforming his whole being. For the first time in two years he felt alive.

After they had been in the church for about an hour Sue asked him what his plans were for the rest of the day. James explained that his car was parked on the other side of Walton Hill and he had intended to walk as far as The Fountain and then back via the Four Stones. "Could I come with you?" Sue asked. "If it isn't too much trouble you could then drop me off at home. My home is only a couple of miles from the car park." James hesitated and then agreed. Why not? He would be glad of the company. A bit like old times with Ann he reflected but then put the thought immediately out of his mind in order not to dwell on the past and to enjoy the present moment.

They set off by heading up Clent Hill towards the Four Stones. It was a steep incline that needed their breath for the upward journey but eventually they reached the top. Here they looked out over the countryside with views as far as the Shropshire Clee Hills and the Worcestershire Malverns. Then they sat down on the grass together. "Did you come here with Ann?" Sue asked. James sensed that Sue had discovered something of what had given him a zest for living – the English language, literature, and an interest in history and walking in the open countryside. "Yes I did," he began, "but I haven't been here for years and I have not felt like going for walks." Sue had also guessed correctly that he and Ann were no longer together and he confirmed this as he continued the conversation. Instead of pursuing details of his time with Ann she asked him what it was about walking that had seemed so special to him. James replied that it was being outdoors, doing something physical but which allowed the possibility of thinking, and also in the company of somebody else to provide mutual enjoyment. It was a short descent to the foot of the hill and then along the road back to the car park. James changed back into his shoes and then asked Sue for directions for the way back to her house. Sue still lived with her parents and when they arrived at the house she asked James if he would like to come in. He was unsure after just a few hours together and he declined. Sue asked him if they could meet up again next Saturday and maybe do the same walk in reverse. James thought for a moment and then agreed to call for Sue at 10 o'clock the following Saturday morning. With this Sue leaned across from the passenger seat and kissed him gently on the cheek. And with this gesture of affection she got out and went into her house.

As he drove back home James went over the events of the day on the hills. He had managed to get himself out of doors and engage in something he had enjoyed a few years ago. This was an achievement.

He had also met someone who knew him and this was encouraging, the beginning of a feeling of belonging. Sue's company had been welcome and their interests matched perfectly. Now he was going to see her again. He was already looking forward to next Saturday. And that farewell kiss...? What was that all about? Was he about to enter a new relationship?

Chapter 5

During the following week work seemed to drag. Saturday seemed at first a long way off but it eventually came. James got himself ready and set off in good time to call for Sue. When he arrived at her house Sue was ready. She looked most attractive in blue jeans, a red sweater and brown walking shoes. She got in the car and they drove to the same car park as the previous week. This time they set out up the hill to the Four Stones and continued towards Clent village. They talked as they followed the route. Sue was keen to know if James had any future plans for a career, his having told her previously that he was at present in a very basic job. After a while they stopped, sat down on the grass and then continued in conversation. They talked about places of historic interest that they had visited and those they would like to visit. Also about books and reading, favourite areas for walks and to which parts of the countryside they felt attracted. Their two minds appeared to be in deep harmony. Sue leant towards James and placed her head on his shoulder. Instinctively James put an arm around her waist. They kissed. The kiss became an embrace and lasted some minutes but then they stood up, becoming aware of other people walking past them on the hills. They made their way past The Fountain and stopped once more at the parish church. Sue looked at James and said "James, I really love being with you. I haven't felt so happy for years. You are wonderful to be with and I hope you feel the same about me." After a brief pause James answered, "Sue, I do love being with you. You have given me a reason for living. After I had finished my studies at university I lost all my energy and when Ann finished with me I lost the will to put my mind to anything regarding the future. You have given me back my interest in life, in people and in the future." With this mutual declaration they went into the church and sat down in silence. After which they looked around the building for a while and then went outside into the churchyard. James turned to Sue and said, "I have just had a clear idea for a future career. I would like to teach the subject I enjoyed so much at university. I am going to find how best to train as a teacher of English." "That's wonderful" Sue exclaimed. "But is that all you have decided about your future?' "Not quite", James replied "I would like to spend that future with you." Sue embraced him and they kissed. Her response to this statement was expressed in the mutual kiss and embrace. After which the uphill route back to the car seemed little more than a gentle stroll.

The End

BLESS THIS HOUSE

Chapter 1

Julie Griffiths was making breakfast when her four-year-old daughter Sarah came into the kitchen. Her husband David had gone to work and her eight-year-old son Matthew had set off for the village school in the company of a neighbour and her children. Sarah sat down at the kitchen table and asked her mother "Who was that man who came into my bedroom in the middle of the night?" Julie stopped preparing the breakfast and replied, "You mean Daddy?" Sarah looked at her mother and then said "No. He was older than Daddy and was wearing old-fashioned clothes. He woke me up." Now Julie was concerned and asked, "Did he touch you to wake you up?" "No. I woke up on my own. He was just standing there. Then he walked through the wall and was gone." Julie tried to say something that might effect conclusion to this conversation. Eventually she managed to say, "I expect it was a dream. You've been watching a lot of stories on television lately and I expect it's something to do with one of the programmes." "No. He really was there. I was asleep and all of a sudden I woke up. I thought Prince might have come upstairs to lie down in my room but it wasn't Prince. It was a man." Prince was the family's dog, a black Labrador. Julie made an effort to get on with her daily routine and so she placed cereal, milk and sugar and a drink in front of Sarah and said "Oh well, eat your breakfast now. You're coming shopping with me this morning and so we need to get a move on."

Why was it, Julie wondered, after a relaxing weekend that Monday mornings always seemed to present difficulties and challenges? In any case, she needed to get on with all that she had planned to do this Monday morning.

The family had moved into this detached cottage some six months ago. It was located in the old part of a medium sized Warwickshire village near the shops, village inn, garage and church. The founding of the village went back centuries and was recorded in the Domesday Book. A chocolate box ideal of a village in Middle England and only a short drive from the larger towns of historic interest such as Warwick and Stratford upon Avon. They had been indeed most fortunate in securing such a home in this location. David, her husband, worked as an accountant for a firm in Warwick and Julie was happy to be here where she had become involved in several village groups in addition to looking after the children. Prince, their dog was also a good excuse to go out for walks and meet people in the village.

Julie said nothing at first when David arrived home but after the evening meal and when the children were in bed she felt that she really must share what Sarah had told her that morning. So she told David and he listened. He too was of the opinion that it had been a dream and so nothing more was said. They did, however, leave their bedroom door ajar when they retired for the night. Morning came and went and Sarah's morning chatter contained nothing out of the ordinary. Julie concluded that that was the end of it.

Chapter 2

The following Saturday, and on all the weekends, the family always took breakfast together. As the four of them sat around the table eating their bacon and eggs, Sarah exclaimed " I saw that man again last night." David and Julie stopped eating and first looked at each other, then at Sarah. David broke the silence. "Where was he? What was he doing?" "Nothing. He just stood there by the bed and then he walked through the wall." Sarah replied. "I expect it's just a dream," David said. Then Matthew joined in the conversation "No. It's not a dream. I've seen him too." Then there was silence. Soon afterwards the children had turned the conversation to where the family might be going today and what activities might be suggested. So the subject was changed and they all got ready for a country walk. Sensing the preparations Prince showed his appreciation by wagging his tail and moving towards the door.

Some half-an-hour later they were all dressed in coats, scarves and wellington boots and Prince was on his lead. They set off through the village and into the fields via a footpath in the centre of the village. About a mile further on they met up with another family with which they had made friends since their arriving in the village, Peter and Susan and their children Stuart and Pauline. The two sets of children chattered and played together among a row of trees and the adults engaged in conversation. After a few minutes Sarah summoned up enough courage to ask "Do you know who lived in our cottage before the last occupants? All we know is that the last couple only stayed about four years." Peter knew something about the three previous sets of occupants as his family had lived in the village for a long time. He could recall being told that none of the previous occupants had stayed more than five to ten years and before that there had been an elderly couple that lived there after the First World War. None of the last sets of occupants had mixed much with the village, had kept themselves to themselves and had not turned up to the various seasonal village events. With this scant information Sarah had to be content as it was time to continue with their walk.

Later that afternoon Sarah made her way into the village to the shop in order to buy some fresh vegetables for Sunday lunch. As the shopkeeper served her, Sarah enquired "Do you happen to know anything about the history of our cottage?" The shopkeeper looked at her with a faint smile and said " Oh, you'll be wanting to know about the old man who walks around upstairs." Sarah froze as she heard this reply. "It's a cottage with a haunting," the shopkeeper continued, "something to do with an unexplained death. But what happened remains a mystery. I shouldn't let it worry you." But it did.

That same evening when the children had gone to bed and they had cleared away the evening meal, Julie and David went into the lounge to watch television. "Oh, you've already turned the TV on!" said Julie. "I haven't been in here since we went out into the kitchen to do the washing up" David replied. "You must have switched it on." He looked at the controls and then at the wall socket. The switch was off. "That's odd" he exclaimed, " It must be an electrical fault". And then he thought no more about it.

The following day, after Sunday lunch, as they sat down in the lounge with coffee, the TV suddenly came on. Nobody was near it and the remote control was still on the side table next to the TV. The children had gone upstairs to play in their bedrooms and Prince was asleep on the rug in front of the fireplace. "All this is beginning to get to me" Julie began "I wonder if this place really is haunted." And she told David about what the shopkeeper had said the previous day. "Don't talk nonsense." David snapped. All the same he did spend a half-hour checking the socket and the TV plug until he was satisfied that they were both in order.

Chapter 3

Two days later in the week, in the middle of the morning as Julie was doing some housework she became aware of an odour in the lounge. It wasn't a cooking smell, nor the smell that lingers when animals live in a house. It was sweet and not unpleasant. Like perfume. But she didn't wear perfume in the week and all her bottles and sprays were upstairs in the bedroom on her dressing table. The perfume smelled familiar. It was like the perfume worn by someone she knew. But who? Then she remembered. Christine! It had been her favourite perfume. Christine who had been at school with her. Christine who had been her best friend. Christine who had been killed in a tragic road crash on the A34 four years ago having been hit by a drunken driver as she returned from a day in Oxford.

Julie went into the kitchen and made herself a strong cup of coffee to steady her upset nerves. When she eventually returned to the lounge the perfume smell was no longer present. In the afternoon she went out for a walk around the village with Sarah and Prince. Near the green she met an older lady whom she knew from the village choir, of which she herself was a member. Sarah was happy playing with Prince with his ball on the green as they talked. Julie ventured to ask her companion "Are there any stories of strange happenings in this village? To do with houses or buildings or people?" Her fellow choir member told her that in the village inn there was supposed to be one room in the accommodation wing that guests would never stay in. They would book a room, and if they were allocated this particular room, within ten minutes of being shown to it they would be back down in reception either wishing to change the room or to cancel their reservation. It is said that those who chose to accept the room allocation reported that furniture in the room 'moved' during their stay.

Apart from this, there was the story about the church.

"And what might that be?" asked Julie.

The woman went on to explain that it was said that there was a curse on the church that extended to any incumbent and principal persons. "A curse? What do you mean?" Julie enquired. The story was that some gipsies had come to the church to see the vicar and had asked him to conduct a funeral for one of their family who had just died. Gipsies tend to keep themselves to themselves and not mix with *gorgios*, that is non-gipsies. However, in matters of religion they are reasonably orthodox and embrace the Christian rites of infant baptism, marriage and death, albeit on their own terms as Christian ministers often discover. On this occasion the vicar had refused to perform the rite. The gipsies went away but two days later on Sunday as the members of the congregation were leaving the morning service and the vicar was chatting to his departing parishioners at the door he noticed a group of gipsies standing midway between him and the churchyard gate. When all the parishioners had left the gipsies came forward and repeated their request. As the vicar seemed to be taking some time the verger and the churchwarden came outside to find the vicar engaged in a lively conversation with a group of gipsies. When the conversation came to an end, the vicar having once more refused the request for a funeral, a member of the group who appeared to be the leader pronounced a curse on the church and on those in front of him, after which the group of gipsies left.

Within the year, quite unexpectedly, the vicar died, the verger was taken ill, confined to bed for the rest of his life and after a few months the churchwarden was committed to a mental institution. Since that time the village has not had its own incumbent, services being taken by a vicar from the neighbouring parish and in addition, apart from services, the church is always locked.

Chapter 4

Later in the evening when David was at home and they were by themselves, apart from Prince who was lying down asleep, Julie recounted her day's findings to David. "Just typical village folklore" was his answer. "All this simply adds to interest in the village.

Without it the place might not appear very much out of the ordinary." Sensing that David didn't seem to want to participate in her own thoughts, Julie let the matter rest. At about half-past-ten when they had just finished watching the news on TV Prince suddenly woke up and started to make for the stairs. He was not usually allowed upstairs, particularly at night and this was unusual. "What is it, boy?" David asked. "Want to go upstairs?" The dog stopped at the foot of the stairs and began to whimper. Then after a few minutes he stopped and lay down again. "Better check the children," Julie said. She went upstairs and after a few minutes she came down again. "Everything alright?" asked David. Julie replied, "Matthew's asleep but Sarah was awake. She said 'that man' walked through her room again. She doesn't seem bothered and she's gone back to sleep." Julie continued, "I'm getting concerned about this. I don't like it. First our home and now today hearing about happenings in the inn and the church. What are we going to do?" "What can we do?" said David "It's not something that we can ring up some company to fix. I expect it will sort itself out. There's probably a perfectly reasonable explanation that we haven't stumbled upon yet". With this last remark everything was shelved for the night. Julie, however, found it difficult to get to sleep.

The following weekend David decided to take the children and Prince to Stratford upon Avon for a boat trip he had promised them some weeks ago. Julie was not keen on boats, or anything to do with being on water for that matter and so she said she would stay at home and find something to do on her own. When the rest of the family had left she realised what a pleasant day it was and thought a short trip in her car might be in order. There was one place not too far away that she had always meant to visit and somehow until now had not got round to it –the Rollright Stones on the Oxfordshire and Warwickshire border. She would drive there, have a look round and be back within an hour or so. That would do nicely.

The Rollright Stones are Neolithic and Megalithic monuments near the village of Great Rollright. According to legend the groups of stones are known as the King Stone, the King's Men and the Whispering Knights respectively. These 'characters' are reputed to have been turned to stone by a witch's curse. The King's Men form a circle that is for most visitors the main interest in the monument. Local folklore says that one is unable to count the stones in the circle accurately. People with dowsing rods often visit the site due to a theory that the stones are situated along a ley line. Pagan groups are said to visit the stones and conduct ceremonies.

Armed with some basic printed information Julie drove off and found the lay-by next to the stones. She parked her car, got out and first went to inspect the King Stone and the group known as the Whispering Knights. Then she turned her attention to the King's Men, that is, the stone circle. She put a donation in the box as requested by a notice at the entrance and went in. She was alone in the circle today.

It didn't take long to walk round the stones. She tried to count them but lost interest and gave up. It was much more interesting to look out over the hills of the Oxfordshire countryside. After about a quarter of an hour she left the circle and returned to the lay-by and her car. Behind her car there was a light grey pickup vehicle with a man standing by the cab smoking a cigarette. He was scruffily dressed, his skin weather-beaten and hair unkempt. Obviously a worker of some sort. To ascertain his age would be problematic, he could be anything between thirty and fifty. The stranger spoke first "Good morning, Miss. Been looking at the stones, then?" Julie replied, "Yes. I haven't been here before. Do you know anything about them?" The stranger seemed prepared to engage in conversation and he continued, "This is a strange place. People seem to be drawn to it. We get some funny types here. People who dress up in robes and dance around the stones. They say there is some kind of magic here but there is also something bad. It's not a place that brings people luck. In fact the opposite." Julie kept questions flowing to ensure that the conversation continued. The stranger talked also about seeing fires lit at Hallowe'en and had heard of strange rituals taking place. On one particular Hallowe'en his brother had seen the fires from his dwelling and had driven up to see what was going on. There were several cars in the lay-by. He parked his vehicle and walked towards the entrance to the circle. He could see people dressed in robes lit up by the light of several burning torches and they were congregating around the stones. He quietly made his way to the entrance gate but he was seen and a man, supposedly the leader of the group, walked towards him waving a sword and quite understandably his brother had hurried back to his car and had driven home.

Feeling reasonably confident in the company of the stranger Julie mentioned some of the disturbances she and her family had experienced recently. What did people do about such things? The stranger thought for a moment and then gave her an answer. "Well, there is a man called Bob Miller who lives two villages away from here. Some people have asked him to come and cleanse the places where things have happened." The stranger also gave Julie a description of how to find this Bob Miller's house. Then Julie thanked the stranger for his time and help, took her leave and drove home.

Later that day, after lunch when David and the children had returned Julie was alone downstairs with David and the children were out in the garden. Julie told David about her morning visit to the Rollright Stones and what the stranger she had met had said. David listened and then asked, "So have you come to any conclusion?" Julie waited a few seconds before she summoned up enough courage to reply, "I think it might be worth seeking out this man whom the stranger mentioned who he thought might be able to help." David was unsure about his course of action and so Julie dropped the subject. For the time being at least.

Chapter 5

Over the weekend there were a few more instances of the strange and as yet unexplained happenings. Sarah saw the 'man' again one night and on one occasion the kitchen radio came on of its own accord. Julie secured another discussion with David about these events and they finally agreed that they would have nothing to lose in speaking to this man Bob Miller whom the stranger at the Rollright Stones had mentioned.

On Monday after Julie had dropped Sarah at the Monday playgroup in the village she took her car and drove to the village where the stranger had said that this man called Bob Miller lived. She found the house and tentatively walked up the cottage garden with flowers on one side and vegetables growing on the other. She hesitated at the front door and then eventually used the knocker. After a short while the door was opened and a man stepped into the doorway. "Yes. What is it, Miss?" Julie explained why she had come. "You'd better step inside" was the answer. Julie followed the man into the living room. It was medium size with a bare wooden table and chairs to match, a sofa and armchairs and an open fire. Bob asked her to sit down. He began "Yes. I can see why you have come to me. I know the house where you live. Some time around the time of the last war the lady of the house died suddenly although she was not very old. Her husband never got over it, stopped working and died within the year." Bob went on to mention the other strange happenings in the village, the haunted inn and the church curse. "Of course that goes on because nothing has been laid to rest," he explained. Julie asked him what could be done about their home and he replied, "I would need to call and come into the house and say some words in each of the rooms." He enquired about children and animals in the family and if he might come when these were with some one else for the half hour he would need. Julie assured him that this was possible and they agreed on a day in the evening. She then thanked him and took her leave.

Later that day she related all this to David who said, "Why couldn't we ask a vicar or someone like that to come here?" Julie reminded him of the situation with the local church and so David reluctantly agreed to fall in with what had been arranged.

On the designated evening the children and the dog were with a neighbour, on the pretext of somebody coming to the house to discuss the redecoration of the children's bedroom and this was meant to be a surprise.

Just after seven-thirty the doorbell rang. There was Bob Miller holding a horseshoe and a sprig of heather. "Tokens of good fortune" he said as Julie opened the door. David asked him if he needed anything and if he would like a drink. He didn't and declined the offer of a drink. He asked which rooms had been the location of the suspected paranormal events and explained that he would need to walk though the whole house with his horseshoe and heather and say some words in the rooms where there had been things happening. They were to accompany him, which they did. He started with the lounge, walked to the kitchen, then upstairs through the bedrooms and finally back downstairs to the back door. In each room he held out his horseshoe and heather, said a few words *sotto voce* and concluded with the Lord's Prayer in the traditional version that includes "Thy" and "Thine". Then he made his way to the front door, shook hands with David and Julie and left. As he did so he turned to them both and said "You'll be alright now. Goodbye."

In the weeks that followed there were no more disturbances and family life seemed to have a peaceful future. That future, however, would be elsewhere, as indicated by the "For Sale" board that was positioned outside the front door.

The End

PLAYGROUND GAMES

Chapter 1

Charles Morgan was watching television mid-afternoon on a day that he had taken off work, or rather he was bored and flicking through the channels with the remote control that he held in his hand. This particular programme on the screen was a selection of old black and white photographs, one of those specialist documentaries about social life and events that had now faded into the distant past. They were pictures of primary school children dancing around in a school playground, engrossed in playground singing games. He listened to the words:

The wind, the wind, the wind blows high
The rain comes scattering from the sky
She is handsome, she is pretty
She is the belle of the noble city
She comes a-courting, one, two, three
Pray will you tell me who it may be?

On the screen the children were holding hands and dancing in a circle around a girl standing in the centre. As they began the second verse Charles could envisage playing this game at his primary school at Wootton Keynes in Gloucestershire all those years ago when he had learnt the game and he filled in the words he remembered, substituting his own name as the children sang:

Charlie Morgan says he loves her
All the boys are fighting for her
Let the boys say what they will
Charlie Morgan loves her still.
He loves her, he loves her
She sits upon his knee
He says "My Darling, won't you marry me?
I love you and you love me
And next Sunday morning the wedding shall be."

Charles let his memory wander back in time. He recalled his primary school days, the pupils in his class, the boys he played with in the playground, their names, which villages they came from and those who were his closest companions during his six years there. Playground games had largely been organised by girls, being an extension of their repertoire of skipping and ball games, the girls usually keeping to corners or well-defined parts of the playground whereas the boys tended to race round over the whole area chasing each other at 'tag' or playing football. So why had the girls' playground games included the boys at all? He was able to remember these singing games, the words and the tunes. He recalled that it was the fact that in many singing playground games it was necessary to have boys included because of the 'pairing off' that formed part of the games. For example, the game called "The farmer's in his den" needed a 'farmer' and a farmer was in those times always male. And in the game that he had just watched on the television each girl when her turn came to stand in the centre picked one of the boys in the circle. This was the reason for the boys' inclusion. Another theory might have been that in those days boys and girls paired off anyway, as boyfriend and girlfriend, then courtship and marriage and the game was a kind of rehearsal for what would follow later in life. But which girl had chosen him? At this particular moment he could not remember. He watched the programme until this particular clip finished and then went back to flicking through the channels until he found an old film and watched that for the rest of the afternoon.

At about half-past four his wife June came home from her teaching job. June came into the lounge and asked Charles how his day off had been and then he asked her how her day at school at been. After this brief exchange they made a mug of tea each and sat down together.

Charles had met June at a party when they were both in their twenties and soon after they were married. Charles was working as an engineer in a large manufacturing firm and June had a teaching post in a secondary school. Now they were in their fifties and although they had moved house a few times they were still in the same line of employment. They had two children, Robert and Patricia, now both grown up and married with families of their own. Charles and June had settled down to middle-aged life together, the mortgage was paid off and the rest of their lives lay ahead of them.

Since the departure of their two offspring they had embarked on more adventurous holidays. In the last five years they had toured America in a hire car, stopping at motels along the route and discovering places they had hitherto seen only in films. They had visited Portugal and the Algarve, toured Italy and managed a Mediterranean Sea cruise lasting a few weeks.

Their interests apart from holidays together were different. June was fond of sport and belonged to the local tennis club and Charles was keen on exploring second hand bookshops and hill climbing. They lived a contented life and enjoyed each other's company.

It was later on that evening when they had finished their meal, loaded the dishwasher and settled down with a glass of wine – a white Sauvignon Blanc for June and a red Merlot for Charles – and they were busy reading their respective magazines that Charles began to think back to his time at primary school in the village in Gloucestershire. He went over the playground singing game once more in his memory. He could visualise his school friends in the circle but he couldn't remember the girl standing in the middle. Who was she? What was her name? Where was she now? She had picked Charles to be her companion in the game and he couldn't remember who she was.

June had finished her glass and suggested a refill. She also suggested they watch another episode of a documentary series they had been following on television. This they did. Then it was time to prepare for tomorrow and go to bed.

Chapter 2

Two more days remained before the weekend and these passed quickly by. After the evening meal on Friday Charles and June discussed what they might do at the weekend as they had no other plans as yet. June favoured a day out shopping in Bath followed by lunch at a nice restaurant. Charles was not overly keen on this suggestion but he had nothing else in mind and it was better than sitting around all day so he agreed. As the evening wore on his memory retrieved more details about his time at primary school. Somehow the scene he had watched on television had been a catalyst in this recollection of memory. He wondered now, at this distance in years if he could dig up anything else from the depths of his memory. Would the school still be there? He couldn't see why not as it had served many surrounding villages and was reasonably large for a village school. Then he had an idea to set his mind at rest. Perhaps they could extend the proposed trip tomorrow and pass by the school on the way home. It would only be an extra hour's drive and then after looking at the school on the way home they could find a nice village pub and have a drink in the garden, or maybe even a meal and make a day of it. Charles said nothing of this during the rest of the evening in case his idea were turned down out of hand. He left the suggestion until the following morning when they were on the way to Bath. June was surprised at this proposed adjustment to their day out that had been mainly for her benefit. "Why have you only now thought about looking up your old primary school? It's over forty years since you were there and you haven't shown any interest before." Charles said something about wanting to look up certain places before he was too old to do so and as this one was relatively close to where they lived he would start with his old village school. There were other places he had in mind, too. This was not true. He was trying to get his quest approved and he began to invent other places where he might like to go –holidays, coastal areas, cities but he got the feeling that he wasn't making a convincing argument. He dropped the subject as they were now approaching Bath and they drove on to the car park and walked into the city. As usual they agreed to give each other a couple of hours on their own and then meet up at the chosen restaurant. June asked Charles what he might do while she embarked on her shopping expedition. "Oh, I think I'll go and walk around the Royal Crescent and then wander over to Pulteney Bridge and the gardens. I'll meet you at 1.30 pm." And with that they went their separate ways.

Charles walked up to the Royal Crescent, a majestic street with a large lawn in front and stayed there for a while. Then he made his way back to the centre, walking down George Street and Broad Street, heading for Pulteney Bridge and watched the water as it flowed over the weir below. Then he entered the Parade Gardens and found a seat where he could spend the rest of his allotted time before going to meet June for lunch. As he sat he played over the playground games in his mind, trying to remember the names of his fellow schoolchildren and his own participation in the games. He recalled most of the names but who had he been paired with? This missing link was not forthcoming and so he watched the water cascading over the weir until it was time to go for lunch.

Halfway through lunch Charles suggested that they should not hurry back home but make a detour through the edge of Gloucestershire and find a pub to relax in as it was such a pleasant day. June had spent a successful morning shopping and had bought a summer dress and a skirt and was therefore agreeable to the suggestion. Shortly after 3.30 pm they walked back to the car park and drove out of the city towards Gloucestershire. The roads were relatively quiet probably because most people who had thought of driving somewhere had already reached their destination and were not yet heading home. They passed by or through the fashionable locations such as Badminton and Tetbury after which they took minor roads. Charles was heading for the village where he went to school and he mentioned to June that as they were quite near to the school they might as well drive past and then he could tick off another place of his list of locations to revisit. They reached the village and found the street where the school was. But something was wrong. Charles stopped the car next to the wall surrounding where the playground had been and stepped out of the car. It was different. The playground had shrunk into a small car park and the school buildings were now a block of apartments. "Is this it?" asked June as she got out of the car. "It doesn't look much like a school." "No' said Charles "It's not the same. I wouldn't have recognised it. The old Victorian building has been converted into flats and the children must go to a larger school somewhere – maybe nearer to Cheltenham or Gloucester. I've had a look. Let's drive on and find a pub." This was his way of concealing his disappointment, to move on quickly before he became depressed and morose. And so they drove on. Within half an hour's drive they found a pub and they sat in the garden with a drink. Not feeling hungry after their late lunch they were content with a glass of wine for June and a Shandy for Charles as he was driving.

June's day had been successful as she now had two new items for summer to go into her wardrobe but Charles was unsettled and had not yet come to a conclusion about what the day had achieved for him. The school building he had expected to find was still there but what he had just seen had in no way helped to refresh his memory. The disappointment in seeing the change seemed to freeze the whole memory process and leave him mentally exhausted. After an hour they drove back home and then spent the rest of the evening watching television.

Chapter 3

During the next week there were several moments when Charles thought about the playground game from his early years in education. The words came clearly back to him. Then suddenly he found he could visualise the girl in the centre of the circle. She was wearing a blue and white summer dress and her name was...Cathy? ... Ann? No! It was Rachel, Rachel Brown. That was her name! Rachel Brown was the name of the girl in the centre of the circle in the playground game. It was Rachel Brown who had picked him for her partner and it was he who had –at least by joining her in the game- consented to marry her. That event had of course not taken place. It was only a game and they were both barely ten years old at the time. He had moved away with his family after he finished primary school and his education had continued elsewhere. But where was Rachel now, he wondered?

Once he had established the name of the girl in the centre of the circle other memories surfaced. Rachel had been in his class right through the school and though at this stage of his life he stuck together with other boys since boys played with boys and girls with girls, Rachel was still one of the girls with whom he had got on well. Rachel had been one of the brighter pupils in his class, much like himself and they had often talked together, had leading parts in school events and gained good marks and favourable comments from the teachers.

As the week took its course and he became immersed in his job, Charles put these memories to the back of his mind. However, they did keep resurfacing and he got the distinct feeling that this was becoming an unfinished business and that he eventually might have to embark on some course of action that would bring things to a satisfactory conclusion. But how would he be able to do this on his own without involving June, who in any case might not be interested in his musings about the past? Would she want to explore things with him? Would she take offence at his trying to trace people from his past? He was unsure of the answers to these questions. He was, however, quite sure that he needed to discover more for his own sake.

A few weeks later Charles received information about a forthcoming three-day conference to do with work that would count as continuing professional development. The location was a hotel in Cheltenham. He felt because he had not had any professional input in the last year he might secure a place on the conference. There was also another reason for his wanting to attend. Cheltenham was in Gloucestershire and no great distance from the primary school that he had attended. Of course he could easily commute from home for the three days but the idea of a residential conference in the summer when he could drive around on his own in the evenings appealed to him. The more he thought about it, the more it seemed like a good idea. Would he be able to convince June that the residential element was a good idea? He thought so and accordingly booked a place for himself. The conference was in a month's time. This would give him just enough time to think where he might go on one of the evenings. The first evening would be taken up with getting to know people and reading up notes and so the second evening had possibilities. As far as he could see from the programme, the second evening was free. He would drive out to his old school and have another look.

How would he find out about the school in the village? He considered where such local information might be available. Apart from looking up websites he seemed to remember June doing some research for school and contacting a town reference library. This could be a possibility. He looked up the Cheltenham library and noted contact details. Then he studied the conference information again and discovered that on the last day the training finished at noon and with this the conference was over.

That was it! He would arrange to go to the reference library at 12.30 on the last day of the conference so that he could find out information about the school in Wootton Keynes. He went online, found details of the library contact and sent an email, mentioning the recent TV programme and to ask if the staff could help him with details about the school. Now he had to wait for a response.

When he got home he told June about the conference that he had booked and that he would be staying in a hotel for two nights. June was not put out as she would be at work anyway but she didn't understand why he couldn't commute each day. Charles explained "Do you know what it's like driving into Cheltenham for a nine o'clock start and then leaving for home at five o'clock? I'd spend ages in traffic. I might as well stay each night as the firm's paying anyway." June answered briefly "Well, you're old enough to please yourself, I suppose" and then nothing more was said.

Within a few days an answer came back from the reference library. They did have information about the school and he would be welcome to meet the archivist at the time and date stated in his email. So that was settled. Now he would just have to wait a few weeks until the date of the conference.

Chapter 4

Driving from home to Gloucestershire some weeks later for the first day of the conference Charles was in an expectant mood, not for learning and discussing professional things but because he hoped to find out more about his old primary school. June had been neither interested nor enthusiastic about his attending the conference. They had said goodbye to each other after an early breakfast and then Charles had departed.

The first day of the conference passed without undue strain. Participants got to know each other in the various refreshment breaks and meal times. Charles phoned home and spoke to June late in the evening. The conversation was brief as June felt tired after the day's work and having got up early to see Charles off she fancied an early night.

Towards the end of the second day of the conference Charles began to make his plans for an evening trip to once more take a look at the school at Wootton Keynes. He decided to skip the evening meal and by 5.30 pm he was driving his car in the direction of the village. On arriving he drove to his former school and parked the car by the wall outside. He got out and took a long hard look at the building. The original structure remained the same and presumably it was the interior that had changed, classrooms and high ceilings most probably transformed into two storey apartments. There were a few additional buildings, blocks of garages on both sides of the original building and in the front what had been a generous sized playground was now a visitors' car park. Where there had been a large field there were now patios and small, neat gardens for the ground floor occupants. Charles tried to imagine where the children had stood in the circle in the playground game but it was too difficult to accurately recall the scene. He stayed for a while and then got back into the car and drove back to the hotel.

The final day of the conference came and went. At midday he said a hurried goodbye to the conference members and drove off to park near the library. This done, he made his way to the library and went to reception to explain that he had made an appointment to see the archivist. A phone call was made and the archivist appeared, a woman probably in her fifties, in a black skirt and white blouse, smart and good-looking, wearing spectacles that enhanced her face and hair. "Good afternoon. Mr Morgan? I am Mrs Baker. Please come this way. I have a folder of items for you to look at." Charles thanked her and followed her to a corner on the ground floor of the library. Mrs Baker was both pleasant and efficient. She had assembled various newspaper articles, official documents and photographs of Wootton Keynes primary school. Not wishing her to immediately leave him on his own Charles asked a few questions about what was on the table in front of him and as he glanced through the set of photographs, one particular picture caught his eye. It had been taken in the playground, evidently for some national celebration and showed a number of pupils in a circle engaged in a playground game! Charles reaction on seeing the photograph was to exclaim, "This is exactly what I have been hoping to find!" "A playground game?" Mrs Baker asked. "Yes" Charles replied "I remember playing these games in the 1970s. I left this school in 1975." "So did I" Mrs Baker answered, "But you gave your name as G. Morgan in your email and I don't remember a G. Morgan when I was there." Charles explained, "My initials are G.C. Morgan. Geoffrey is my first name but I have always been called by my second name which is Charles." "You're Charlie Morgan!" exclaimed Mrs Baker. "And who are you, then?" asked Charles. "Rachel. I was Rachel Brown." "Rachel. You are the reason I have been trying to find out about the school playground games. I saw this programme on the television. Then I started to remember the playground games at Wootton Keynes. I remembered "The Wind blows High". I could visualise my school friends in the circle but I couldn't at first remember the name of the girl in the middle. Then after some time I remembered your name." "Not Brown any longer. I married. Now I'm Rachel Baker." "Yes, I realise that. Do you remember that in the game you picked me and I said I was going to marry you?" Rachel did remember and they continued in conversation talking about their lives after primary school, who they had married, the children they had brought up and what they were doing and where they were living now. After almost an hour they had shared everything that seemed appropriate to the occasion. "So what will you do now that you have solved the mystery of the girl in the middle?" Rachel asked Charles. "I suppose it closes a chapter that was as yet unfinished in my memory" was his answer. "I can go back to living my life as it is now." Rachel thought for a moment and then said "I didn't regret picking you in that game. I always thought that you were one of the more interesting and intelligent boys. But then you moved away." "Yes, I did" Charles replied "But now I must move on. It was a real pleasure to see you again after all these years."

And with that they parted. Charles had found a kind of closure to his quest and he had to be content with this.

He made his way back to his car and drove home deep in thought. What might his life have been if his family had stayed in Gloucestershire? Would he have settled there? Would he have married a local girl? Rachel? These thoughts would stay with him for the rest of his life and would remain in his memory as things that might have been, not as things that might be. With such thoughts he headed home to the world that was his and to the future that would inevitably be controlled by his present life.

June arrived home shortly after Charles. As she walked into the kitchen she asked him "What was your conference like?" Charles gave this answer "A lot of people in a circle concentrating on one in the middle. A bit like a playground game."

The End

ALL IN THE MIND

Chapter 1

Teresa sat in her room at her desk looking out of the window. The garden outside was full of bright and beautiful colours in the summer morning sunlight. Flowers were resplendent in the border around the lawn and cherry trees were in blossom. Birds were feeding at the bird table on the edge of the lawn and as yet the sun had not quite reached the oak garden bench under her window.

This morning she had been late getting up and had only just dressed. She had not eaten breakfast and had not felt like doing anything until lunchtime. In fact, she didn't feel like doing anything at all. She had felt like this for weeks now. At least it seemed like weeks but she was unable to retrieve from her memory just how many weeks it had been.

This was a fact of life in a psychiatric hospital. Each day was much the same, a daily total of hours interspersed by mealtimes with nothing to do except sit around with one's thoughts. There were, of course, activities and group sessions available to fill the time and form part of the therapy but for Teresa, as for many other patients these facilities appeared uninviting, lacked imagination and stimulation, were not tailored to the needs of the individual and represented the institutional programme of events that could be offered or afforded at any one time. The participation in groups was in any event voluntary.

So the days passed by in the same vein, one got up when one

liked, ate or missed breakfast, sat around till lunch, interacted briefly with staff and other patients in the dining room, sat around till tea time and then after a few more hours one went to bed and tried to sleep. There were a few interactions with staff concerning the giving of information or medication and that was all. One could go into the garden or sit in the lounges – Teresa avoided the latter with the televisions transmitting their basic diet of daytime programmes watched in silence by other patients, but she favoured the garden where it was usually possible to be alone. The garden was away from the ward corridors that were frequented by certain patients who spent their day constantly walking up and down, bombarding the staff with impossible demands and annoying fellow patients.

Teresa felt herself to be a prisoner with no privileges, unable to choose what she would like to do each day, restricted to the institutional regime and unable to leave the ward for the world outside.

Because of her section, Teresa was not yet allowed to leave the ward either escorted or unescorted and so there was no possibility of going into town for shopping or to sit in a café, to go for a walk or to meet people. If she made progress and cooperated with her treatment plan these privileges would come in time but she didn't wish to cooperate and so everything seemed a distant possibility.

Chapter 2

Teresa had been admitted to the hospital three weeks ago. The circumstances of her admission were complex but to state things as succinctly as possible the story was this:

Teresa went through school and on to university but then dropped out in her second year largely due to a failed relationship with Ben, a fellow student. She came home to her parents and there were tensions concerning her perceived failure and inactivity and also with her younger sister Hazel's academic success with which she felt both compared and judged. Teresa showed no interest in anything and just sat around at home. Family tensions and arguments became a regular feature and one day she just packed a few belongings and left home.

She gravitated to the nearest large town and ended up sharing a house with four other women. She found work in a local café in order to make ends meet. In her spare time she hung around with a motley collection of people she had met, a mixed group of unemployed and part-time employed twenty and thirty somethings. They listened to music, drank alcohol, took drugs and had casual relationships with one another. Then Teresa began to report sick for work, her attendance became erratic and she lost the job. Debts mounted and she could not pay her rent and so unable to face her responsibilities or her fellow housemates she left one night and wandered the streets, sleeping rough. It was at this stage of her life that she was found by the police and subsequently admitted to the hospital.

Around midday Teresa left her room and walked along the corridor towards the large area where staff worked and where other patients hung around besieging the staff with questions that usually received no satisfactory response. Teresa found Jane, a member of staff with whom she related reasonably well and asked her about her impending review in two days time. Jane replied that the consultant would not be here this week and so the review had been postponed for a week. Now Teresa would have to stay confined to the ward for over a week before a decision might be made to allow her some leave. Dejected and disappointed she walked back to her room.

Chapter 3

Teresa lay on her bed throughout the whole afternoon. She thought that she might be able to sleep and thus forget everything about her life. Sleep, however, was not forthcoming and she struggled with the different thoughts that vied for attention in her mind as she lay on the bed. Questions swirled around in her head "Why am I here?" "Why is life like this?" "Why am I no good at anything and no use to anyone?" "Wouldn't everyone be better off if I just weren't here?" Once these questions had surfaced they would not go away, they just stayed in the forefront of her thinking. She was mentally exhausted and consequently felt no inclination at all to do anything except just lie on the bed.

The rest of the week followed a similar pattern. She got up late, missed breakfast, ate a hurried lunch and then lay on her bed for the rest of the day either ruminating or sleeping.

At the beginning of the following week staff had become concerned about Teresa's inactivity, seclusion and refusal to participate in any of the daytime sessions and so after the review with the consultant –which did happen this time- a twice weekly appointment was made for her with the psychologist in the hope that this might have some therapeutic benefit.

Chapter 4

In the afternoon of Friday of that week a member of staff came to call for Teresa in her room to say that it was time for the meeting with the psychologist. She was then escorted to the psychologist's room.

As Teresa entered the room the psychologist stood up, walked towards her and announced in greeting "Hello. You must be Teresa. My name is Caroline and I am the psychologist. Thank you for coming. Please sit down."

Caroline explained that they had an hour together and they would meet twice a week for a total of up to ten sessions. She checked that Teresa understood which days and times they would meet. Teresa listened to all this without making any comment. Then Caroline asked Teresa if she would like to tell her something about her life and how she was feeling at the moment.

"What do you want to know?" Teresa asked. "I don't *want* to know anything in particular" Caroline answered, "It's simply that you have the opportunity to talk about anything you like and my role is to listen and be attentive." This last remark took root in Teresa's mind. "Some one who might listen rather than tell me what to do. Some one who might help me to sort out all the thoughts in my head. Some one who might actually want to see things from my perspective and help me through this present pointless existence". And so Teresa began to talk and Caroline listened.

Teresa explained that her life seemed fine until half-way through university. When she met Ben she lost interest in her course and then Ben lost interest in her and abandoned her for some one else. Her tutors didn't attempt to find out why her academic performance had diminished and gave only criticism and warnings. Teresa had given up studying for Ben and now he had given her up and so she stopped going to lectures. To avoid being sent down she left her course of her own accord. Her parents were less than sympathetic of her coming home, things were said about how much they had done for her and now she was throwing it all away and in addition there was constant comparison with her younger sister who was destined for a successful university course after the summer. Rather than continue to face all this tension Teresa left home. Life after this had been unsatisfactory as she had fallen in with people who had little interest in permanent relationships and just hung around drinking alcohol and doing drugs. The job she had during this time was boring and after repeated absences she was sacked. It was after this point when she was sleeping rough and saw no point in living that she attempted to end it all and in the process was discovered by the authorities and admitted to the hospital.

Caroline listened to all this, only interjecting with short questions in order to ensure that Teresa kept talking and telling as much of her story that she felt able to do. The story took up most of the session. Teresa felt, possibly for the first time in her life, that some one had given her undivided attention, without comparison or judgment and more importantly, she had been heard. This was the beginning of the therapeutic alliance between patient and facilitator. Caroline sensed that Teresa might be prepared to work with her and so she asked "We could have a look at the things you have talked about in the next session and then see if we can work out how you might go on from there, that is, if you are in agreement." Teresa nodded in assent. "Well," Caroline said, "we won't start on this today but before our next session I would like you to think about what is most important for you at this moment and we can start with that next time." And with that the session ended.

For the rest of the day Teresa thought about her meeting with Caroline. The session had been quite the opposite of what she had expected. She had thought that the psychologist would give advice and encourage her to get more involved in the ward programme of activities and cooperate with staff requests. Instead, Teresa had done most of the talking and she now felt better for having been heard. She was already looking forward to the next meeting. She considered Caroline's suggestion that she might formulate what it was that she wanted in her life at the present and so she began to occupy her mind with these thoughts as she lay on her bed in her room.

Chapter 5

Over the next few days Teresa continued to think about what it was that was important to her. At first she had not thought that anything at all was important to her. After all, she had decided that her life was no longer worth living and she had tried to end it. This was why she was here in the hospital. Since her admission she was in the care of the hospital staff and her treatment would be geared to helping her continue her life, even if she didn't want this to happen or to cooperate with the treatment. Non-cooperation had been a choice she was able to exert in not attending any therapy activities. But now she had in fact attended one session with Caroline. Could this have been some neutral ground, an opportunity to reconsider what life for her was all about? Perhaps Caroline's suggestion for her to ascertain what was most important for her might be a chance to reconsider. Before meeting with Caroline the most important thing for Teresa appeared to be that she should cease to exist. "Was there an alternative?" she asked herself. "What had her life been about anyway?" She thought of family, school, university, and the relationship with Ben, her housemates and the crowd with whom she had begun to hang around and eventually came to the conclusion that there was one thread in her life that joined all the various stages – it was the need to belong. She felt the need to belong to people or some one and for this belonging to be healthy, mutual and permanent. She held on to this revelation and kept it in focus for her next meeting with Caroline.

Chapter 6

Caroline had only half-expected Teresa to do any serious thinking and come up with anything with which they could work together. At the next meeting when she asked Teresa if she had discovered any thoughts about what was most important for her, Teresa replied, "The most important thing for me is the need to belong." This was a good start. They talked about what this might entail and then Caroline suggested that they might attempt a few sessions of Cognitive Behavioural Therapy to help Teresa find alternative ways of appraising life's situations and events. Teresa felt that anything was worth a try and so they began to work together.

They went back to each significant event in Teresa's life where the event had caused her to have unhelpful thoughts that in turn had led to unhelpful behaviour and consequences. For example, when Ben finished with her she concluded that no one else would ever want to have a relationship with her and that she was incapable of being loved. As a consequence she gave up her studies and left the very society at that time in her life –students of similar age and intelligence – where belonging could be both a possibility and a reality. Caroline helped Teresa to see alternative ways in looking at life events and how to explore alternative, helpful thoughts in order to engender helpful behaviour and consequences. Over the next few sessions they did this for each of the main stages in Teresa's life –family, university, friendships – where the need to belong had become stuck or had not been realised.

As the sessions progressed Teresa began to understand how she had never considered alternative courses of action for the different events in her life and because of this they had ended in disaster due to her unhelpful assessment of what she had perceived in each event.

If her family compared her to her sister then that was because she was different and not defective. If Ben left her for someone else then that could be that he was not the right one for her, not that she was a failure in a relationship and would never be able to enter a relationship again. If the people she had associated herself with after university were a dysfunctional group with little regard for permanent friendship then she could attempt to find a more positive group to belong to.

Her attitude towards herself began to change, she decided to do something about the need to belong and joined one of the activity groups on the ward. In the art room she rediscovered a hitherto neglected talent, that of glass-painting that she had taken up years ago while at school. The member of staff in the art room encouraged her and her pictures were noticed and admired by other patients who were regulars in the art room. Teresa began to visit the art room most days and made friends with some of the other patients. This at least was the beginning of belonging.

Chapter 7

A few days later, Jane, the member of staff with whom Teresa related well, came to Teresa's room to say that she had a visitor.

Teresa made her way to the reception area and saw a woman standing there. She was wearing a light brown coat and white trousers and appeared to be about thirty years old. As Teresa approached the woman turned and Teresa immediately recognised her as Jan, one of her former housemates. "Hello Teresa," Jan said, "I've come to visit you if that is what you would like." Teresa answered her without hesitation "Of course. Thank you. The staff will book you in. You'll have up to an hour." Jan was duly booked in and together with Teresa they were escorted to a day room, left alone in the room with a member of staff sitting outside in the corridor, able to observe through the window.

Jan explained that a few days ago, while she was in town in her lunch hour she had been approached by one of the people with whom Teresa used to hang around before she was admitted to hospital. The man who approached her said that he thought that they both knew Teresa and if this was the case then he could tell Jan where Teresa was. He had this information from another patient who had been on Teresa's ward who knew that Teresa had belonged to the same group as he. Such communal intelligence is not unusual in the world of those who hang around not working and doing drugs.

Jan had seen no harm in admitting that she knew Teresa and the man told her where Teresa could be found. He gave the name of the hospital and the ward. Jan found out the visiting times, phoned the ward, explained that she was Teresa's housemate, made an appointment and here she was.

At first, Teresa was overcome by the fact that someone had taken the trouble to follow her up her disappearance. It was another sign of belonging, that erstwhile elusive state that she had said was most important to her.

For the hour that was permitted for the visit Teresa told Jan how she had come to be in the hospital and explained that although she had tried in her life to fit in somewhere, nothing seemed to work and she had come to believe that she herself was the cause of all her problems.

Now, only recently she had found some hope in the sessions provided by the hospital psychologist and she was beginning to comprehend what might have gone wrong and how to go forward from this point.

Jan listened for a long time and then asked Teresa "So you are not going to end it all now?" "No, I'm not. I want to make a fresh start" was Teresa's reply.

As their time came to a close Jan asked Teresa if she come and visit her again, at the weekend, and Teresa agreed. Then they walked back to reception, Jan said goodbye, and she left.

Chapter 8

The following day was another session with Caroline, the psychologist, who was pleased to see how enthusiastic Teresa was in her therapy. Teresa had now grasped the principle of challenging her dysfunctional thoughts, seeking alternative ways of thinking about events that had occurred and then experiencing more positive effects in behaviour and consequences. They would continue to meet until the ten planned sessions were completed.

The weekly review with the consultant went well and as he was satisfied that Teresa was making good progress he arranged an allowance of daily leave from the ward, two hours escorted leave for a week and then, if all went well, two hours unescorted the following week.

On Sunday afternoon Jan visited once more. They spent an hour in the garden together and talked about what they had both done since last time they had met.

Jan was pleased that Teresa was receiving some leave and she promised to come again next Sunday to see if Teresa's leave had now been modified to unescorted leave each day.

The rest of the week passed smoothly. It was good to get out of the ward in the afternoons for the daily two hours leave. Jane was assigned as the escort and that was a real bonus. During the course of the week they went round the shops, had a coffee together, visited and sat in the parks and went round the abbey, patronising its tea rooms for tea and cake. Teresa was beginning to look forward to what seemed to be the start of a new phase in her life.

The consultant was pleased with reports from the art room and ward staff about Teresa's progress and unescorted leave was duly scheduled for the following week.

Jan called again on Sunday and suggested that they might meet up in town on Saturday afternoon in the Abbey Tea Rooms where they could talk together over tea and cake. Teresa readily agreed.

Chapter 9

The weekend seemed to come around again quickly and on Saturday after lunch Teresa left the hospital and walked to the Abbey Tea Rooms to meet Jan. They met outside in the abbey grounds and then went into the tearooms for tea and cake. After they had been there for about an hour Jan asked Teresa "Have you ever been into the abbey? We could visit and walk round inside if you like." Teresa was delighted at the idea and said, " No, I've never been inside. I'd like that." And with that they left the tearooms and entered the abbey.

Teresa was surprised at the sheer size and beauty of the interior. There were three aisles in the nave and several side chapels leading up to the quire and sanctuary. They were not alone in the building. There were a lot of people – individuals, couples and families either walking around looking at the various parts of the building and also some people just sitting in silence or lighting a candle at the votive light stands. Teresa felt a tangible peace in the abbey and walked round in silence. After a while Jan asked her what she thought of the abbey and Teresa replied, "I can feel peace. The possibility of being alone but also to be able to see others around you. There is a sense of belonging."

"I come here on Sunday mornings to a service" Jan explained "I too feel as if I belong even though I don't know many people here. I still know a lot of them by sight and that makes me feel part of a community."

They looked around for a little longer and then Teresa paused at one of the votive candle stands, lit a candle and stood there for a few minutes in silence. Then it was time to leave. "Could I meet you here tomorrow for the service?" she asked Jan, to which Jan said that she could and then they went their separate ways.

The next day Teresa met Jan at the abbey and they attended the service together. Afterwards Teresa said to Jan "I am really beginning to think that I belong somewhere now. I have valued your friendship and now I have also found a place where I can feel some peace. I feel that my life is taking a turn for the better."

Teresa's life did indeed take a turn for the better. Over the next weeks a date was set for her discharge from the hospital and Jan suggested that Teresa come back to share the house with the others and move back into her old room. There was even a chance of a job at Jan's place of work.

The need to belong was gradually becoming fulfilled. Other stages would follow in due course.

The End

OXFORD REUNION

Chapter 1

As the airport coach neared the city terminal Norbert Steinberg felt himself gripped by a sudden wave of apprehension, almost fear. This was unusual for a man such as he in his late thirties and it had been twenty years since he had last made this journey. In those days it had been by train and ferry. Norbert was a capable individual, not unused to organising travel or even his life for that matter but this trip was partly one of nostalgia although no particular outcome was anticipated.

He had first visited Oxford while in the Unterprima –the Lower Sixth would have been the British equivalent- at his boys' grammar school in North Germany. His English teacher had, through an agency, arranged for a number of interested pupils to stay with British families for a period of three weeks in the summer holidays. Norbert had applied for this venture and was duly allocated a family in the city of Oxford.

Norbert knew nothing at all about Oxford but with the help of his teacher and a city guide he had managed to discover where his host family lived in a side street a little to the north of the city centre.

When the day of departure came Norbert and several other boys assembled at the local railway station and travelled via Cologne and Brussels to Ostende, where they took the ferry to Dover. Most of the group journeyed on to London and then via the various rail termini to their final destinations. Norbert and two others left Paddington for Oxford, where upon arrival they were met by their host families and driven to their respective homes.

Mr and Mrs Butler were in their forties and had two children, a boy of twenty called Jonathan who was at a college of the University of London and a seventeen year old girl called Janet who was in the sixth form at a local girls' grammar school. Their home was a medium-sized four bedroom Edwardian detached house with a garden and a good-sized lawn fringed with tall tress and only ten minutes walk from the edge of the city centre. Norbert's hosts explained that Jonathan was away in France for the summer vacation and Norbert would be occupying his room. Norbert had been travelling all day since an early hour and with this in mind the Butlers had delayed their evening meal until his arrival. Now he was here they would be able to get to know each other over a simple meal before bedtime, after which they all retired for the night.

On the first day of his stay the Butlers had arranged for Janet to take Norbert into the city to get a feel of the various places of interest. At ten o'clock he presented himself ready and he and Janet set off in the direction of St Giles. Janet pointed out the various colleges on the way and then after passing Balliol they turned into Broad Street to visit Blackwells bookshop. They walked past several other colleges and the Radcliffe Camera before ending up in the Covered Market where they stopped for a coffee. Norbert took an instant liking to Janet. She was about his height, slim, with short blond hair and blue eyes, attractive and frequently smiling as if she enjoyed company. She was a perfect companion.

They bought sandwiches and fruit before leaving the market and then Janet led the way to the University Parks where they sat down and ate their lunch.

Norbert could hardly believe his good fortune in being placed with the Butler family. They were splendid hosts and their daughter was intelligent, pleasant and attractive. If the three weeks continued like this he would be extremely content for the rest of his time in Oxford.

Chapter 2

On several days Norbert was left to himself to organise his time and he spend such days visiting the colleges, walking by the river or sitting in the meadows reading. Each day he was expected back to the house for lunch and dinner and so the various periods of time that he spent on his own were manageable. At the weekends Mr Butler had time off work and there were family outings planned to Abingdon, Woodstock and Stow on the Wold in the Cotswolds. Janet would also be included in these excursions and this pleased him greatly.

Janet was like Norbert, half way through her upper school course and she was studying 'A' level French, English and History. Norbert wished she were studying German, for then at times they could have used his native language. However, it was in order to improve his command of English that he had come to Oxford and so this made no great difference to his stay. He talked with Janet about school, interests, friends and family. Janet had a keen interest in walking and in the countryside and it was her strong hope that one day she would move out of the city environment and embrace life in a more rural setting. In the autumn she would be making an application to go to university to study French and then train as a teacher.

Chapter 3

At the beginning of the second week Janet asked Norbert what his plans for the day were and he replied that he hoped to go down to the river and the meadows. Janet asked if she could come too and Norbert readily agreed. Janet therefore arranged with her mother that they could take a picnic lunch with them and return later in time for the evening meal. This was agreed.

Around midday saw Norbert and Janet in the University Parks choosing a spot for their picnic. After they had eaten Janet lay down on the grass in the warm sun and said to Norbert "I'm glad you came to stay with us. This is what I like best of all, just lying in the open air on the grass in sunny weather. It's like being in the country, which is where I want to be." "I like the country too" Norbert replied "It is a village where I live."

"Perhaps we could take a bus to Woodstock and spend some time in the grounds of Blenheim Palace by the lake" Janet suggested. "We could go Friday morning. I'll ask my mother." "Oh that would be very nice" Norbert replied.

On Friday morning Norbert and Janet took a bus to Woodstock and went to Blenheim Palace. They did not visit the house but made their way to the area surrounding the lake. Here they spent all day, walking around the park or sitting in the shade on the grass. Lunch was once more a picnic brought from home. After lunch Janet lay down on the grass and stretched herself out in perfect contentment. Norbert sat beside her and looked at her as she lay beside him. Janet was young and attractive with a pleasing figure, her blond hair falling around her cheeks and her eyes closed in the warmth of the sun. He experienced a feeling of completeness and pleasure. Without opening her eyes Janet spoke "You know, Norbert, I really like being with you. It's almost as if we were going out with each other." Norbert's grasp of English idiom was insufficient for him to realise the full significance of Janet's remark and so he answered "But we are going out. We came out here from Oxford."

Towards the end of the afternoon they packed up their things and walked back to the exit from the park. As they walked Janet slipped her arm through Norbert's and drew herself close to him. She said, "Please don't think that I am a flirt, Norbert. It just that I like being with you." Unsure of how to react, Norbert kissed her on the cheek and said, "I think I love you." Janet gave no reply and so they left the park and took the bus back to the city. Norbert's mind was in turmoil. What had happened to him? To Janet? He was unsure. He did, however, have one more week to find an answer. Tomorrow was Saturday and no doubt the family would have some idea of what they might all do together. He could wait till then.

Chapter 4

On Saturday morning when Norbert came down for breakfast it was obvious that something other than a family outing together had been planned. Janet was dressed in travelling clothes and her case was packed and standing in the hall. Mrs Butler explained that Janet was going away to a summer school in Durham for two weeks and was leaving by train that morning.

Norbert was devastated. He had looked forward to a continuing relationship with Janet and now she would not be around for the remainder of his stay. After breakfast a taxi arrived outside the house and the family gathered to wish Janet a pleasant time in Durham and all that Norbert managed was to utter the words of goodbye. He returned to his room despondent. The final week would seem empty without Janet with whom he had fallen in love.

Nevertheless the week did pass but time seemed to drag very slowly and without Janet the days seemed like an endurance test. Eventually the time for departure to Germany arrived and he bade farewell to the family, thanking them for his time among them.

He was desperate to get in touch with Janet and so after the summer holidays he wrote a letter to her. A week later he received a reply. It was a short letter thanking him for his letter and a few lines about Janet's entering the upper sixth in the coming week. Nothing more. Was it all over then? All the time that they had spent together? The mutual interests and affection? Norbert felt unsure about everything and feared the worst –that it was all over. Had it not been for his own return to school and settling into the Oberprima he would have just hung around and moped.

A few weeks later at the beginning of October he wrote again. This time there was no reply. November and December passed and still nothing. By the New Year he gave up all hope of any further communication. So it was indeed all over. His first love had run its course and come to an end but he would never forget Janet.

Chapter 5

Norbert's coach was now making its way around the ring road on its way to Gloucester Green coach station. He was thirty-seven now and on holiday from his work with an insurance company in Cologne. After he had left grammar school he had embarked upon business studies and over the years he had worked in banking and insurance. He had never married although he had several girlfriends over this period in his life. None of the relationships lasted more than a few months. He had been content to live a bachelor life in a rented flat, taking holidays over the years as a solo traveller both in Europe and worldwide. In all this time he had never been back to the United Kingdom, now his holiday destination for the next three weeks. He planned to visit London, for him as yet unexplored, and rather than staying in the capital he preferred to stay some way out with the possibility of day trips. Hence his choice of Oxford with rail connections of about an hour to the capital.

On arrival at Gloucester Green Norbert made his way on foot to his hotel, unpacked and studied the itinerary that he had compiled for the next three weeks. His list of places included not only London but also Stratford Upon Avon, Bath, Cheltenham, the Cotswolds and of course Oxford itself. He would easily keep himself occupied for three weeks.

After the first seven days he had been to London twice and in a hire car he had visited Bath and Cheltenham. He thought he should now relax a little from travelling around and spend some time in Oxford. He walked to the Carfax, the old centre of the city, and then to the Covered Market where he stopped for a coffee. Then he proceeded via Turl Street and Broad Street towards St Giles. He decided to have lunch at Browns. As he left the restaurant after a leisurely meal he remembered there was a route past Keeble to the University Parks. Suddenly it all came back to him. Walking the parks with Janet, lying on the grass in the sun and that first kiss. It was as if he had never left that moment even though it was separated by twenty years. His thoughts were now in turmoil. In choosing Oxford as a base from which to explore England it had not been his intention to relive the distant past. He had simply chosen Oxford because he knew his way around and the location was central to what he had planned to do. Now his thoughts turned to the time spent twenty years ago and of his time in the company of Janet.

He began to wonder if the Butlers would still be living in the same house. Also what might have happened to Janet? No doubt she would have married and be living elsewhere, even abroad since she had studied languages.

For the rest of the afternoon he wrestled with the idea of going to the house where the Butlers had lived to see what he could discover and thus attempt to settle his thoughts. It was now late afternoon and a call in the evening might not be a good idea and so he determined to try tomorrow in the middle of the morning. He now found it difficult to pass the time before the following day and he eventually decided to spend the evening watching a film in the small eclectic cinema in Walton Street. After the film he went back to his hotel and tried to sleep. He woke several times during the night, his mind constantly active, but at last he managed several hours before it was time to get up.

Chapter 6

After breakfast, Norbert went for a long walk around the city before making his way to the street where the Butlers had lived. He found the house, looking much the same as it had done two decades ago, walked up the drive and then with a degree of immense apprehension he rang the bell. There was a long pause that seemed to him to be an eternity and then just as he was about to ring a second time the door was opened. An elderly woman stood in the doorway "Yes?" she enquired. "Excuse me, but are you Mrs Butler?" Norbert asked. The woman hesitated for a moment and then said, "Yes. I am. Can I help you?" Norbert answered " My name is Norbert Steinberg and I came to stay with you twenty years ago for three weeks. I am on holiday in Oxford and wanted to see if you still lived here." "Oh yes! Norbert! How wonderful to see you again. Won't you come in? My husband is in the garden."

Norbert was led through the hall and the kitchen into the garden where Mr Butler was sitting on the patio reading the newspaper. After introductions tea and biscuits were provided and the three of them caught up on each other's news. Norbert told of his time since school, Mr Butler was now retired and involved himself in the garden and Mrs Butler occupied herself with the house. Eventually Norbert could no longer contain his curiosity and he ventured to ask after their children. Jonathan had made a successful career in computers, was married with three children and lived in Reading. Then there was a pause. "And Janet?" Norbert asked. Mr and Mrs Butler looked at one another and then Mrs Butler explained, "Janet finished school and went to university to study French and during her year abroad she met a French boy, also studying at the university. In their final year they married. Janet came home briefly after the end of her course and then went to live in France. All seemed well for a year but then they separated and divorced. Janet stayed in France for a while and then returned to England. She got a teaching post in a private girls' school and is still teaching there.

There followed another pause and then Norbert broke the silence "Do you see her often?" Mrs Butler said that they saw Janet a few times a year but she never stayed long, at most overnight and left the next day. "And where is she living now?" Norbert asked. The answer was that Janet did not live far away at all and had a small house that she had bought in Moreton in Marsh in Gloucestershire. Norbert asked if he might be able to visit Janet and the Butlers thought it would be possible. They provided him with the address. He stayed for a further half hour and then took his leave, thanking them for their hospitality and once more for the time he had spent with them all those years ago.

As Norbert made his way back to his hotel he thought through the practicalities of a surprise visit to Janet. It was school term time and she would be involved in teaching and school activities all day and into the early evening and so he decided that a Friday around seven in the evening might be a good time to call. Tomorrow was Friday and he made the decision to drive to her house then.

Chapter 7

Norbert felt that time was passing very slowly all through the following morning and afternoon. He tried to occupy himself with walks around the colleges, frequent stops for refreshment and a leisurely late lunch. Then at about six o'clock he got into his hire car, joined the home-going traffic and drove to Moreton in Marsh.

The town was a pleasant settlement along the Fosse Way. With accurate directions provided by the Butlers he soon found the street and the house. For minutes he sat in the car wondering just what he was doing here. What was it that he hoped to achieve?

Would Janet be in? And if not, would he try again? Would she recognise him? Eventually he made up his mind to knock on the door and see what transpired. He summoned up enough courage, got out, headed for the front door and knocked. There was a pause and then the door was opened. Norbert was face to face with Janet. There was no mistaking her from her appearance. She was dressed in a skirt and blouse, her hair was still blond and short and apart from looking a little older she was instantly recognisable.

Norbert spoke first "Hello Janet. Do you remember me? I am Norbert Steinberg and I came to stay with your family in Oxford twenty years ago." Janet gasped either with shock or surprise, Norbert was unsure which. "Norbert. Yes, I remember you. What are you doing here?" Norbert explained his holiday based in Oxford, his meeting with Janet's parents and how they had given him her address. Janet appeared to understand. "It's been so long. Twenty years, you say. You'd better come in and have a drink. Tea or coffee?" Norbert followed Janet into the kitchen where she made tea and then they sat down in the lounge. Norbert told Janet about his life after school and then it was Janet's turn to say something of her life. She gave a brief account of university, her time in France and now as a teacher in the Cotswolds. Then she asked him "How long are you staying in Oxford?" Norbert replied that he had two more weeks before his return. Janet asked about his plans for the remaining time and Norbert mentioned the places he would still like to visit. He wondered if he should dare to ask, then he hesitated for a minute and said "You wouldn't like to come with me to Stratford Upon Avon either Saturday or Sunday and show me round, would you? I could buy lunch for us." Janet hesitated and began to make excuses about preparation for school but eventually she said, "Yes. I could come with you tomorrow if you come here for ten o'clock. Will that suit you?" Norbert agreed and after he had finished his tea he left and drove back to his hotel. As he drove he wondered what would come of the day out together. Would it now bring closure to the friendship of twenty years ago? Would it be just another place ticked off on his itinerary? He decided that he would not try to think too much on that score and so when he arrived back in Oxford he went to bed early to be ready for the next day.

Chapter 8

Janet was ready when he called at her home on Saturday morning. Dressed in white trousers and a light blue tee shirt and with sandals on her feet she looked both smart and attractive. They set out for Stratford Upon Avon and managed to park without difficulty. During the morning they did a circular walk along the Old Tramway and then crossed by the Chain Ferry and walked back into town. They had lunch at one of the many pubs in Sheep Street. Afterwards they sat on the grass by the river and watched people enjoying themselves, eating ice creams or waiting for boats by the jetty. Janet lay back on the grass and after a while she said to Norbert "Can you remember lying on the grass in the University Parks twenty years ago?" Norbert said that he could. On some kind of impulse he said to Janet "Why don't we go there now and then afterwards I can drive you home. It's not all that far." Janet thought for a second and then said, "I'd like that. Let's go now."

They returned to the car park and in just over an hour they had parked in a side street and were walking towards the Parks. Janet found the very place where they had enjoyed a picnic all those years ago. They sat down on the grass and then lay down with their faces turned towards the almost cloudless sky. Norbert asked her "Do you remember the last day that we spend together here?" "Yes," said Janet and she leant over him and kissed him on the cheek.

It was as if for twenty years time had stood still.

The End

CHANGING TIMES

Chapter 1

Imogen Sayers was standing with a group of school friends waiting for the train home from school on the station platform at Adamsdale. It was almost four o'clock and the local stopping train that carried most of the schoolchildren home would soon be due. Like all fifteen-year-old schoolgirls they chatted together, talking about school, homework, teachers and boys. At this time of day the talk was mainly of boys, many of whom were also standing around in groups on both platforms of the station. The opposite platform for trains down to London and the one where Imogen stood being for trains coming from the direction of the capital, some two hours away by rail.

Imogen's group and the others from her school were not the sole educational establishment represented. There were also both boys and girls from the town's grammar school waiting on the platforms. Pupils from the two schools were easily distinguished by their respective uniforms. Imogen's school, the town's secondary modern, had a uniform consisting of grey and blue clothing whereas the grammar school uniform was mainly navy blue except for white shirts and blouses.

Rarely did the pupils from the two schools mix with each other while travelling even though several knew each other and even lived near to each other in the same town or village. It was almost as if there was an unwritten code of behaviour that required everyone to keep to one's own school community. At times there were instances of tension and conflict but these soon passed. The situation did however, not prevent the different pupils assessing the attractiveness or otherwise of the pupils from the other school. Boys would discuss which girls they thought attractive and girls would rate the eligibility of the boys on a predetermined scale. Not one pupil paired off or even sat next to a pupil from the other school. Grammar school girls wanted grammar school boys to sit with them, or at least sit in their carriage and the same was true for pupils from the secondary modern school. To cross this social divide would be to compromise one's own chances of success with one's own school colleagues and this was both unthinkable and was certain to lead to adverse consequences.

Despite these conventions Imogen kept looking at a group of three grammar school boys to her left, being careful not to look too long in order not to attract observations from her travelling companions. These three grammar school boys were older than Imogen, probably fifth form. It was the one in the middle of the group that had caught her attention. She had noticed him before at this time of day but he was never on the morning train that she caught on the way to school. She had also never seen him in Perrybank where she lived. Suddenly the station bell rang out announcing the arrival of her train. Pupils gathered up bags and satchels and looked in the direction of the anticipated train. Imogen stole another glance at the group of the three grammar school boys. Then as the train pulled into the station she saw two boys taking leave of the boy who had caught her eye. He was evidently not about to board this train. That was the reason that she had never seen him on her train in the mornings. Her trains in the mornings and evenings were local stopping trains and the evening one only went as far as her home station in Perrybank. This boy obviously had a final destination further along the line and now would be waiting for the express that arrived later. While processing this train of thought Imogen got into a carriage with her friends and travelled home.

Chapter 2

The following week was half-term and Imogen spent the time with family around the house and garden and meeting up with her friends in town. They met up in a local café frequented by several of her fellow pupils. The holiday passed all too quickly and then it was back to school once more.

Just before four o'clock on the last day back at school Imogen was again waiting on the station platform at Adamsvale with her friends. She glanced around and saw the same three grammar school boys waiting a short distance from her. She looked again at the one in the middle of the group. He seemed quieter than the others, possibly more intelligent she thought, and he had a smarter appearance both in his uniform and in his looks. The shrill note of the station bell rang out and a minute later the local train rounded the bend heading towards the platform. As the train drew into the station Imogen and her friends made ready to board. To her amazement all the three boys she had been watching made ready to board, too, and they did so.

Once on the train, Pat, one of Imogen's friends said that the train was more crowded than usual because the express had been retimed much later and as a consequence this train would be going on further in order to accommodate waiting passengers. This then was why the boy that Imogen had noticed had also got on with his friends. Not wanting to wait longer he had boarded this train and he obviously lived at its revised final destination, in Castleborough.

The following morning when Imogen and her friends got on the train the same boy was already sitting in the carriage they had chosen to occupy. The morning express had presumably also been retimed and now this particular grammar school boy would be travelling both to and from school on the same trains as Imogen. This was indeed most fortunate. Would anything perhaps ever come of this opportunity? Now Imogen would be able to travel to and from school on the same train as this boy who had captured her attention. She made up her mind to go one stage further in her endeavours and attempt to travel daily in the same carriage as his.

This was tricky in the mornings as the train had three carriages. Imogen would have to surreptitiously look out to see which carriage this boy was in. She need not have worried on this account as it soon transpired that he always travelled in the first carriage of the train. Imogen therefore encouraged her friends to board the first carriage each morning and then to sit near to where the boy and his friends were seated. She watched the three boys during the short ten-minute journey to Adamsdale. Her opinion had not changed. This one boy was without doubt the most interesting in the group. But how was she to get to know him? The issue was solved that very afternoon. Imogen's friends had stayed late at school for sports activities and she was waiting on her own on the platform. After some minutes the grammar school boy she had noticed walked onto the platform without his friends. He also was travelling alone today.

As the train drew into the station Imogen headed for the nearest carriage and as she boarded the train the grammar school boy got in after her and sat down opposite her. As the train set in motion she became aware of the boy looking at her basket with its cake tin. Without prompting the boy suddenly asked her "Have you by any chance had Domestic Science today?" Imogen replied, "Yes, I have. We had to bring ingredients to make a Victoria Sponge. Would you like to see it? " "Yes please" was the answer. The boy congratulated Imogen on her excellent cake and then went on to say that at his school it was only the girls in certain sets who continued with Domestic Science to GCE 'O' level. Imogen asked him which subjects he was taking for 'O' level. He said he was studying English, Maths, Sciences, Geography and French. They continued to talk about school right up to the point where the train slowed down as it came into Perrybank. "This is where I get off. It's been nice talking to you" Imogen explained. As she stepped down onto the platform and was about to close the door she turned to the boy and said "By the way, my name's Imogen Sayers." "And mine's Ian Milner" was the answer. With that she closed the door and soon afterwards the train departed.

Imogen kept rehearsing Ian Milner's name as she made her way to the bicycle shed and then home from the station. She could hardly wait for tomorrow to see if this initial encounter might flourish. She considered the practicalities of attempting to travel to and from school on the train in Ian's company. She usually travelled with her school friends and Ian with his. For Imogen to attempt to travel with Ian seemed a logistical impossibility. Still, she lived in hope.

Chapter 3

For the rest of that week Imogen travelled with her friends and Ian with his. To attract undue attention to Ian would only have encouraged gossip and speculation on the part of Imogen's friends. At the beginning of the next week an opportunity did in fact present itself in that on the return journey from Adamsvale Imogen got into the same carriage as Ian and found herself facing him and his two friends. After about a minute Ian spoke and asked Imogen if she had done any Domestic Science that week. She replied that she hadn't and to her amazement and delight Ian continued the conversation talking mainly about school. Imogen's friends looked on with interest, straining to hear what was being said. All too soon for Imogen the train drew into Perrybank and Imogen said goodbye. Once on the station platform her friends bombarded her with questions. How did she know Ian? Did she fancy him? What was he talking about? Why was a grammar school boy interested in her? Imogen avoided much of the answers in that she said she had to collect her bicycle and hurry home today. Soon she was alone once more.

Two days later, alone again on her return journey, as Imogen stepped onto the platform at Adamsvale she saw Ian waiting on his own. They started up a conversation as they waited for the train. In the course of this Imogen found out where Ian lived. He lived in Castleborough with his parents and a sister. "Do you ever come to Castleborough?" Ian asked. "Oh, yes", Imogen answered "I come to the pictures. There are four cinemas in Castleborough and it's better than Perrybank for shopping." Ian asked her "Do you like seeing films?" Imogen explained that she usually went to the pictures about once or twice a month with her school friends usually to Adamsvale but as there were only two cinemas there she personally preferred to go to Castleborough as there was a better choice of films. By this time the train was drawing into Perrybank and Imogen got up, ready to alight. As she opened the carriage door Ian asked hurriedly "Would you like to come and see a film with me sometime?" "Oh, yes!" was all that Imogen managed to say in reply before the train was ready to depart. After which the cycle ride home seemed to take no time at all. With boundless energy she pedalled swiftly towards home feeling as if she were cycling on air.

Chapter 4

The following day Ian was not on the train and Imogen had to endure the comments and taunts of her fellow travellers regarding 'that boy you spoke to'. The school day seemed to Imogen unusually long and the lessons held little interest for her. Eventually the final bell sounded and pupils streamed out of the school gates heading towards transport or home. As Imogen reached Adamsvale station she became aware of a grammar school boy walking towards her. It was Ian. "Hello. I caught the later train this morning as I had a dental appointment in Castleborough. Do you still want to come to the pictures?" Imogen said yes but she didn't manage to utter anything further as Ian's friends joined him at the same moment. As the train drew into the station they all got into the same carriage. Opportunity for conversation with Ian was not possible during the journey and soon the train was drawing into Perrybank. As Imogen turned to say goodbye Ian pressed a small envelope into her hand. She closed the carriage door and walked along the station platform. Then she stopped and opened the envelope. Inside was a piece of paper on which were written these words *"Meet me at the Odeon in Castleborough this Saturday at one o'clock. Ian."*

So it was real. She had a date. Her friends had also seen the note being passed to her. "What did he give you? What does it say?" They asked. "Oh, he just says why he wasn't on the train this morning. He went to the dentist." Imogen answered. Pat said "Gosh. He really must fancy you. And a grammar school boy as well. What do you think of that?" In order to avoid further speculation Imogen said she had to get her bicycle and hurry home as she had been told to get back as soon as possible today. And with that she walked to the bike shed, collected her bike and rode home.

Chapter 5

The following day was Saturday. Imogen chose carefully what to wear- skirt, blouse, jacket, and shoes. Smart casual and not too formal. Then she spent the whole morning doing homework in order to take her mind off the rest of the day and what it might bring. Shortly before twelve o'clock she cycled to the station and caught the twenty minutes past twelve train, arriving in Castleborough at twelve thirty-five. Then she walked down into town to Friars Place where the Odeon cinema was located. As she was approaching the cinema she caught sight of Ian. He was arm in arm with an older girl. Imogen froze on the spot with shock. What was going on? She wanted to run back to the station and go home. Had Ian meant to invite her to make up a threesome with him and his girl-friend? Was the idea of seeing films the only common interest? As these thoughts raced through her anxious mind she tried to think what she was going to do, but then the decision was made for her. Ian had seen her and together with the girl on his arm he walked up to Imogen. He spoke first "Hello Imogen. Thanks for coming. Let me introduce you to my older sister Jane."

Imogen almost burst into tears with released tension but she somehow managed to utter a greeting and to shake Jane's hand. "I'm so pleased to meet you, Imogen" Jane said "Ian has told me about you and I wanted to meet you. Now I am going to leave you both together as I'm going shopping in town." With that Jane was gone and Imogen and Ian were alone together.

They bought their tickets and took their seats in the circle. A short film and then the feature film followed the inevitable adverts. In the interval Ian bought ice creams. They settled down for the second half of the film. Some few minutes after the start of the second half Imogen felt Ian's arm lightly placed around her shoulders.

The arm stayed there until the end of the film and Imogen felt the welcome warmth of his touch. On leaving the cinema Ian suggested they walk down to the river and they walked towards the bridge and sat down on a bench overlooking the river. Ian drew Imogen closer to himself and kissed her. She returned his kiss. Ian said, "I'm glad the railway timetable was revised. Otherwise we might never have met each other.' "Me too," Imogen answered, "It's the best timetable revision I have ever known."

The End

RHINE DISCOVERY

Chapter 1

Colin Sanders looked at the clock in his office in the County Education Department and ascertained that it was nearly one o'clock. It was time for lunch. The May weather was particularly pleasant and warm so he decided to take his lunch box and flask and spend the hour on the banks of the river just across the road from the building where he worked. Colin put his papers away, left the building and walked across the road towards the river. He crossed the grassed area between the car park and other buildings and chose a bench on the riverbank overlooking the boathouse on the opposite bank. As he opened his lunch box he watched the swans as they swam to and fro under the town bridge. He poured himself a cup of coffee from his flask and as he waited for his drink to cool his mind went back in time to the events of the last ten years.

He thought of Lynda whom he had first met at grammar school. For the first three years they had been in different sets but in the fourth form they were placed in 4A, the top set and therefore destined to learn their subjects together up to the GCE 'O' level examinations. In the sixth form there was one subject – English – that they studied together and this contributed to their discovery of feelings for each other. In addition to English Lynda studied Geography and History whereas Colin opted for French and German. It was in that lower sixth year at the Christmas dance that they spent most of the evening together and discovered that they liked each other. In the weeks after the dance they went out every two weeks or so to dances or to the cinema. Then Colin was invited to Lynda's home and soon he became a regular visitor. Their love for each other –for this is what it was – continued to blossom right up to the end of the upper sixth and lasted all through their time at university. Colin read French at Exeter and Lynda English at one of the London University colleges. They kept in touch with each other all through the terms and were together during the vacations when they continued to spend time with one another. Each summer they went camping in various areas of the country, an activity they could both afford on their university grants and casual work locally, Colin in a factory and Lynda in a shop.

After their days at university Colin and Lynda found employment locally. Lynda worked in the county library department and Colin had employment with the education service. At the end of their first year at work they decided to find a flat and live together, which they did.

They spent their weekends shopping, going to the cinema and walking in the surrounding countryside. In the second year of their life together they started to go on holidays abroad. One Easter they had a week in Paris, one summer two weeks in the Austrian Tirol and in the following year a week on the shores of Lake Como in Italy. They also had a holiday in the Canary Islands. Life was pleasant, their work was enjoyable and a happy future together lay ahead of them.

Or so Colin thought. It was last November, six months ago, when he came home from work at the end of the week that he entered an empty flat. Lynda usually arrived home first but on this occasion she was not there. Her coat was not in the hallway and so Colin assumed that she was still in town probably shopping for the weekend. Colin made himself a cup of tea and sat down in the lounge. An hour passed and Lynda had still not come back. He got up and walked through to the bedroom to change. There on the pillow on Lynda's side of the bed was an envelope. Colin opened it and read;

> "Dear Colin
> Our thinking that we could live together was a mistake. I had expected more from our relationship and now I have found someone else who can provide me with this and so I have left to be with him. Please don't try to get in touch. Thank you for the time we were together.
> Yours, Lynda."

Colin read the note again, put it down and then walked through the flat opening cupboards and wardrobes. All Lynda's clothes and personal belongings had been taken away. Bedding, towels, kitchen items and crockery were all there, as of course were all the clothes and things that belonged to him. He went back into the bedroom, picked up the note again and sat down on the bed holding Lynda's final communication to him. He felt numb, confused and desolate. What had been so wrong that their relationship had come to an end like this? They had known each other well for a long time, almost eight years. He could not recall any time during that period when they had not enjoyed their time together. Nor was there ever anyone else for either of them, or so he thought. Obviously now for Lynda there was someone, but not for him. What would he do now? There was actually nothing at all to do. It was over. Life had to go on, for the present time, alone.

Chapter 2

This had happened at the weekend on a Friday evening. Instead of planning time with Lynda Colin would now have to discover how to spend weekends on his own. The flat was rented in his name and the only car they had was his. So he had accommodation and transport but no companion. Not feeling up to making a meal for one he left the flat, bought a takeaway and returned to eat it. As he sat in the dining room eating he began to think what he would do now. To try to contact Lynda was futile and would just take up a lot of time with no results. He still had job, car and flat. His income was enough to manage on and so the only issue now was his own personal life.

It was in the area of living alone, yet having mutual friends and family that Colin now felt unsure, not being able to imagine how the future would unfold for him. If Lynda had come to the conclusion that Colin could not give her a life that was fulfilling then what did this say about him? Was he then a failure? Was he perhaps incapable of a sustained life with another person? His thinking was quite naturally one-sided. He was, like most people in a similar situation incapable of assessing the facts from the other's point of view. He simply came to the conclusion that he had not lived up to Lynda's expectations which is what she had written in her note.

It was late November, with Christmas only a few weeks away and Colin thought of all the seasonal events that he would have enjoyed in Lynda's company. As they had no children they would spend the Christmas period with their respective parents. That would no longer be the rule. Colin resigned himself to the fact that he would be visiting only his own parents this year. Gradually he would have to inform friends and family hat he and Lynda were no longer together. He also felt that he should make some decisions about the things that he and Lynda had done together. He thought he might still patronise the same restaurants and cinemas but not continue with the walking group that they had joined together.

The weekend passed slowly in isolation and then it was time to go back to work.

Now it was six months since all this had happened. Colin had stayed in the flat and continued to work in the education office where his colleagues were more interested in the daily routine and their own lives rather than his change in circumstances. He had spent Christmas with his parents who lived in the Cotswolds and he had continued to visit them every other month for a weekend. They seemed glad to see him even without Lynda. Colin still had friends in the town where the flat was situated but some of those with whom he and Lynda had spent time were now no longer part of his social contacts. Many of these had been couples and Colin felt uncomfortable as a solo item within such gatherings.

As he sat by the river in his lunch hour he thought of what he might do this summer. He had put in for two weeks leave at the end of July and he thought about the idea of taking a holiday abroad. Why should he not enjoy himself and go somewhere? A solo traveller was not an oddity and the only disadvantage would be the extra charge for a single room supplement. He decided to see what might be available before he went home that day. Later he left the office in time to call in at a travel agent and in very little time he had booked a week on a Rhine cruise in Germany. This was for him an unexplored country and he had heard and read about the spectacular Rhineland scenery. The idea of being part of a group yet having his own cabin appealed to him. He would be able to participate with activities or to do things on his own. He made his way back to his flat feeling both satisfied and encouraged by his decision to do something different.

Chapter 3

When the first day of Colin's holiday came he travelled to Heathrow airport, met the tour representative and others in the group and within a couple of hours he found himself on a flight to Cologne. On landing at Cologne airport the group moved through passport control and customs and on to a coach that took them to the cruise ship that was waiting for them. Colin studied the members of his group. There were about thirty all together, some couples, a few were friends together and a few solo travellers like him. On boarding the ship they encountered the other groups on board, Dutch, French and Americans, making up a total complement of around two hundred passengers. Colin found his cabin located on a middle deck, comfortably equipped and with a small balcony that pleased him greatly.

Just before dinner there was the inevitable welcome cocktail meeting for all on board. At dinner, and for all subsequent meals in the restaurant, passengers were seated at circular tables laid for eight guests. These tables were allocated to guests for the duration of the cruise. At Colin's table there were two couples, two friends and one solo traveller in addition to himself. They offered their introductions and then ate their meal together. After dinner, most people explored the ship or went briefly ashore to see the part of Cologne near the river. Colin consulted the seven day programme for the cruise and noted that the ship sailed tomorrow before breakfast for Cochem on the Moselle. This would be a full day sailing.

The following day passed quickly, the scenery enduring the interruptions of morning coffee, lunch, afternoon tea and dinner.

Cochem is a town on the Moselle on a twenty kilometre long bend, settled by the Celts and later by the Romans. Its main attraction is the Reichsburg castle with foundations going back to the eleventh century. The castle visit would be on the next day after arrival. After breakfast on the following day the first event was a walking tour of the town continuing up the steep path to the castle. As Colin's group toured the castle he talked to several of the other passengers. One young woman, one of the people at his dining table on the ship, attracted his attention. She seemed to be more interested in the history of the place and asked the guide several questions whereas most of the group just followed the guide waiting for the next stop on the tour.

Colin ventured to ask the young woman, whose name he knew as Gwen Jones from their introductions at dinner on the first evening, the question "Are you very interested in history?" "Oh yes" was the answer "I teach history at a grammar school." After this brief exchange they walked around the castle together. Colin asked Gwen questions about the historical period and Gwen gave a satisfying answer to each one of his questions. In Gwen Colin found a pleasant companion and they stayed together for the rest of the tour. After lunch on the ship they sailed on to Trier, the oldest city in Germany founded by the Celts and then conquered three hundred years later by the Romans who named it The City of Augustus after the emperor.

At dinner that evening Colin managed to sit next to Gwen. Following the meal there was a folklore evening in the main lounge to which everyone was invited. Following the performance most of the passengers retired to their cabins but Colin and Gwen were not tired and decided to go on deck for a while. They looked out over the city and Colin asked questions about its history. They talked for some time and then returned to their respective cabins for the night.

The programme on the next day began with a city tour that culminated with a visit to the Roman Amphitheatre. The group was then given free time until lunch on the ship and the afternoon sailing to Boppard on the Rhine, another town of Celtic origin fortified later by the Romans.

It was on the following day that they reached Boppard and after a short stop they continued along the Rhine to Rüdesheim. They passed through the Rhine Gorge with the Lorelei Rock where legend tells of a siren figure who lured fishermen to their deaths on the rocks below, and sailed past fairytale castles with names such as "Katz" and "Maus".

After dinner that day Gwen suggested a walk into the town to sample the evening atmosphere of the various wine cafés for which the town was famous. Colin and Gwen found a table in the renowned Drosselgasse and ordered a bottle of local white wine. Colin asked Gwen about her job as a teacher. Gwen taught history which she had studied at Cardiff. "So are you then originally from Wales?" Colin asked her. "Yes. I was born in a small village in the Brecon Beacons where my father had a farm. My parents are still there." Then it was Gwen's turn to ask Colin where he came from and what work he did. Colin told Gwen that he came from a village on the edge of the Cotswolds and after specialising in languages in the sixth form he studied French at Exeter before entering the education service. By this time it was after half-past ten and so they finished their bottle of wine and made their way back to the ship. Here they said goodnight to each other and returned to their cabins.

The following day was the last of the cruising days as the ship had to make the return journey to Cologne. They would probably arrive overnight and then after breakfast it would be the departure for the airport and home.

Chapter 4

On the last full day Colin was up early and went onto the sun deck. Within a few minutes he was joined by Gwen. "Do you mind if I sit with you?" she asked. "Be my guest. I just thought that as this is the last day of sailing I didn't want to miss any of the scenery" Colin replied. They sat there until breakfast was announced and then went down to join their fellow passengers at the breakfast table.

There were several activities planned during the day but Colin and Gwen made a mutual decision to attend just one or two and then spend the rest of the day on the sun deck as the ship retraced its journey through the Rhine Gorge, the junction with the Moselle and on towards Bonn and Cologne.

Between activities and meals they talked and asked each other questions about themselves. Colin talked about his school and university life, the village where he was born and grew up in the Cotswolds, and his present work in education. Gwen spoke of her school and early life in Powys and of her time at Cardiff University. She was still living in South Wales teaching history at a grammar school. They found that they had a common interest exploring countries and the history attached to them. Colin's love of languages and Gwen's interest in history seemed to complement each other.

On the journey to Cologne the ship once again made a brief stop at Boppard for passengers to have a last opportunity to go ashore before continuing the journey. Colin and Gwen took advantage of this concession, walked ashore and made their way to the main attraction in this small town, the church of St. Severus. They looked around inside, sat for a while in the pews and then as they left, Gwen slipped her right arm into Colin's left arm. They looked at each other with affection and so returned to the ship.

After dinner that evening they both went to the sun deck to watch the scenery and the sunset. As they stood together by the railing Colin put his arm around Gwen's waist. She turned towards him and they kissed. He felt the warmth of her body as she drew closer to him. "Thank you for coming on this holiday" Colin said. "I'm glad I came. I met you" was all that Gwen said in reply. They spent two hours together embracing, kissing and watching the sun disappear below the horizon before eventually going down to their cabins. Tomorrow would be departure and so Colin said "Can we see each other again after the cruise is over. I would like that very much."

Gwen gave him her answer "Yes. We must exchange contact details. I have five more weeks' holiday before the next term. Will you come to see me?" Colin explained that he had one more week's leave. "I'll come and see you as soon as we are back. The day after we get home." With that they walked downstairs. As they turned at the foot of the stairs to the cabins Colin looked at a poster he had not noticed before. It had a view of the Rhine Gorge and underneath were the words

Discover Yourself
Discover the Rhine

Colin smiled.

The End

FOREIGN EXCHANGE

Chapter 1

It was the second day of the school exchange visit to a similar secondary school in the twin town in Germany near to the border with Holland. The two schools had been running an exchange for some years now. The British pupils went to Germany around the time of the Easter Holidays and the German pupils made the reciprocal visit at the end of the summer term, after the period of examinations. This year the British group numbered some forty pupils aged 15 to 17 years old, accompanied by four members of staff, two male and two female. Each pupil had a pen friend and the host families provided accommodation. The accompanying staff would stay with their foreign colleagues.

Chris Walker, one of the male British teachers studied the programme for the day. The pupils were to accompany their pen friends to their lessons and the British staff were free to go to whatever lessons they liked to experience how teaching was conducted in a German school. Chris taught French and Spanish and so as a language specialist he decided to join an English class to see how this was taught.

He found an English class for the first lesson of the day and as he walked in he was at once struck by the layout of the desks, positioned around the sides of the room with small groups in the centre, quite unlike the usual rows of a British school. The member of staff, a female teacher was dressed in what one might call 'Smart casual' – in her case smart trousers and a short-sleeved blouse. He had already noticed the more informal attire of the German staff members. For the men, no suits or jackets and ties and for the women not a single skirt or dress to be seen.

The female teacher walked up to Chris and introduced herself in English "Good morning. My name is Ursula Winter. Welcome to my English lesson. Please take a seat wherever you like." Chris also introduced himself and took a seat at the back of the room.

He was most interested in the manner in which the lesson was conducted. The teacher delivered the whole lesson in English, even to the extent of the explanations of grammar and vocabulary. The pupils were not allowed to use German at all. This method of direct teaching in the foreign language was new to Chris. He asked himself whether he would be able to conduct a lesson using this method. He admired the skill of Ursula Winter who also had a pleasant manner in handling the pupils. She seemed to be more like a friend to them than a teacher. She held the interest of the class right up to the end of the lesson. Then she gathered up her briefcase and made her way to the door to go to her next class. As she did so she asked Chris where he would go next. Chris explained that his subjects were French and Spanish and Ursula directed him to where he could sit in on these subjects. Before he moved on he asked her "Could I perhaps sit in another of your English lessons later today? I found the teaching technique most interesting." Ursula answered " Of course. Meet me at room 211 on the second floor at 12 o'clock." With that they moved to their next lessons.

The exchange group was in Germany for 10 days. Two weekends were to be spent with the hosts and the weekdays were a mixture of attending school lessons and some outings by coach to places of local interest. As the German school day was between the hours of 07.30 and 13.00 all afternoons and evenings were with the hosts. Chris had accommodation with Klaus Meyer, a married male member of staff who taught English and who lived in a nearby village. From this location there were woodland walks and a bus service into town and so Chris could plan his own time without imposing on the family.

At 12 o'clock Chris found room 211 and waited for Ursula Winter to appear. The previous lesson had just come to an end and the teacher left the room, bidding a "Guten Tag" to Chris as he left. Then Ursula appeared and they went into the room. Chris was captivated by the way Ursula taught her class. She had their full attention and the pupils were eager to learn and to respond to her questions and assignments. This lesson was about a day visit to London. Chris could easily identify with this. About halfway through the class Ursula turned to Chris and asked "Mr Walker, do you know London? If so, perhaps you could tell us something about the city?" Chris said that he did and that he had lived and worked there in his first teaching post. He stood up at the front of the class, gave some information about the capital and then invited questions form the pupils. He answered the typical tourist questions such as "Have you met the Queen?" but there were other things the class wanted to know and he answered their questions as fully as he was able. He had no idea how long he had been teaching the class when the bell rang and the pupils began to pack up and leave. It was the end of the school day and yet it was only one o'clock. All that remained now was for him to thank Ursula Winter and say goodbye. Chris had enjoyed sitting in on her lessons and also he had enjoyed her company. She was attractive and lively, yet professional and efficient, possibly like all German teachers, Chris thought.

Tomorrow and the next day Chris, his English colleagues and their pupils would not be in school. These days were reserved for outings, one day with the German pen friends to Cologne and another day just for the British groups to another location.

Chapter 2

The outing days passed off without any issues and then it was back to school attendance for the remainder of the week. Chris spent the first of these days in school sitting in on Spanish and German lessons but on the last day he had decided that he would like to attend a double English lesson taught by Ursula Winter. This he did. As he listened to her delivery of the lesson and watched her as she engaged with the class he realised that he was becoming more and more attracted to her as a person and not just as a teacher.

At the end of the school day Chris was sitting in the staff room where there was one other man sitting opposite him, whom he assumed was another member of staff. A short while afterwards the staff members started coming into the room in preparation for their departure home for the weekend. Ursula Winter was also among them. As she entered the room the other man who had been waiting with Chris stood up, walked towards Ursula, gave her a discrete kiss and then they left together. Chris felt devastated. She had not thought of Ursula being attached, but she obviously was, and that was that.

He spent the weekend with his host family. They took him on Sunday to the Möhnesee and its dam, a huge reservoir landscaped for walking and boating and which had also been breached in May 1943 by the RAF in the "Dambusters' Raid". Apart from the place in the dam where a repair had been made there was nothing to suggest that this area was anything other than a local beauty spot.

On the following morning Chris, his colleagues and their pupils all assembled in the schoolyard ready to board the coach for the homeward journey. The German pen friends and some members of staff were also present, Ursula Winter among them. She came up to Chris and said "Thank you for visiting my lessons Mr Walker. Goodbye and have a safe journey " to which Chris managed to say thank you and goodbye. Ten minutes later they were on the way home.

Chapter 3

That was five years ago now. Chris had not been involved since in the school German Exchange partly because he taught neither German nor English but also because he had declined staff invitations to be part of it. This was largely due to his disappointment over finding out that Ursula Winter was not unattached.

In the intervening years he had continued to teach at the same school and although he had originally lived alone in his own semi-detached house on an estate near the school, for the last year he had been involved in a relationship with Vicki, a fellow teacher at his school. Vicki taught Art. Chris had got to know her at staff functions. Then their friendship extended to going out for meals and to local theatres together. One evening in a restaurant Vicki told Chris that she was going to have to move out of her rented flat at the end of the month and as yet she had nowhere to go. Chris suggested she could live with him and Vicki readily agreed. She moved at first into the spare room but as the relationship intensified they ended up sharing a bedroom. They enjoyed being together and for Chris this seemed the beginning of a romance that he hoped might continue into something more permanent.

This, however, was not to be. In the Christmas holidays Vicki told him that she had secured a new teaching post in the North of England and that she would be leaving at Easter, which she did. Vicki moved out of his house and out of his life. She thanked him for his companionship and for providing her with a place to stay, explaining that she would now be embarking on a new stage in her life with new surroundings and new people.

Consequently, this year, since the start of the summer term Chris had been living alone. He soon adapted into what had been his former lifestyle and he found plenty to occupy his time at work, this being the season of public examinations.

As the examinations period progressed, one day Chris was checking the summer term events on the staff notice board –Sports Day, Cricket and Tennis fixtures, and – he had almost forgotten, the annual visit of the School German Exchange pupils. His thoughts went back to the year when he too had taken part. There was also a notice underneath to say that a volunteer member of staff was now needed urgently to accompany the group on a couple of outings. Nobody seemed to have offered for this task. Chris thought about his and then before he went home that day he put his name forward to help in this task.

On the day that the German Exchange group arrived, late in the evening, all the pupils with pen friends in the group, all host teachers and those staff helping with outings assembled to greet the arrivals. The coach arrived and the party disembarked. Pen friends were reunited and staff met their hosts. There were four German members of staff, two male and two female. One of the females Chris recognised as Ursula Winter.

The various staff members introduced each other. Chris approached Ursula who at once said to him "Hello Mr Walker. How nice to see you. I was wondering if you were still at this school." Chris returned her greeting "Hello Fräulein Winter. Yes, I am still here. In fact I will be coming with the group on the outing we have planned for you." And with that the whole group moved off to their accommodation.

Chapter 4

The first outing was two days later. Chris had set lessons for his own classes and was looking forward to a day away from the classroom. When the German group had boarded the coach they set off for Warwick Castle. Chris was the accompanying British teacher for the trip with the responsibility for general assistance and admission tickets. He found on boarding that Ursula Winter had chosen to sit in the front seat and as he needed to be at the front he sat down beside her.

On arrival they had a brief tour of the castle and then the group was allowed to explore on their own. Hosts had provided packed lunches and there were a couple of hours allowed for the rest of the visit. Ursula asked Chris if she could walk around with him, as he seemed to know the castle quite well. They walked along the Ramparts, climbed Guy's Tower and looked at all the exhibits including the Great Hall and State Rooms. Eventually it was time to return to the coach and back to school. The next day would be spent in school at lessons and then there was one more outing planned before the weekend.

On the following day as Chris was about to go to teach his first class he was approached by Ursula Winter. "May I come and sit in your class?" she asked. "It is a French class", Chris explained. "That's alright. I have been learning some French" Ursula replied. "Well, please join me then," was Chris' answer.

In the afternoon Ursula came back to the room where Chris was teaching for the last lesson of the day. At the end when the pupils had left she stayed behind and they talked. Ursula was staying with one of Chris' female colleagues who taught German. However, this colleague was away at the weekend and Ursula would be alone. She asked Chris if he could suggest any local attractions to visit. "I'm not sure what you might have in mind" Chris began, "I remember that when I sat in one of your classes five years ago that you were teaching about London, but I would imagine that you have been there already." Ursula replied, "No, I haven't. I have always wanted to go there. Would it be possible from here? Not too far to go?" "It's not far by train" was Chris' answer. "I am free this Saturday. We could go together and I could show you around." Ursula paused and then said, "Yes. I'd like that."

Chris arranged to meet Ursula at the town's railway station on

Saturday at eight o'clock. He said that he would work out a list of different places to visit. Then Ursula left to go home with her host colleague.

Chapter 5

On Saturday they met at the station, bought tickets and waited for the train. Ursula was wearing white trousers, a cream blouse and a short light blue denim jacket. She looked very smart, Chris thought. They managed to get window seats opposite each other and talked as the train made its way to London.

They were pleased to see the bright sky and to feel the warmth of the summer sun as they stepped off the train at Euston. Now it was a question of where to go first. Chris made the decision to go first of all to St Paul's Cathedral and after a short Underground ride they emerged into the open to see the towering structure of the cathedral in front of them. Inside they marvelled at the lavish interior and walked around in amazement. Seeing a sign to the Whispering Gallery they paid the fee and climbed up. From here one could see the whole inner structure and down below, the seating area. There were not many visitors in the gallery and so it was possible to send a whisper all the way round and hear it as it came back.

On leaving St Paul's they found a cellar restaurant and enjoyed an early light lunch and a glass of wine. Then they made their way to Buckingham Palace and Hyde Park. After the splendour of the Palace and the inevitable crowds no doubt hoping to catch sight of some royal personage the Park and the waters of The Serpentine brought an atmosphere of relaxation, serenity and peace. They lay down on the grass in the warm sun. Chris hesitated for a while and then summoned up enough courage to ask Ursula "What is your boyfriend doing while you are away in England?" Ursula was startled at this question but she answered, "Oh, you mean Carl. You saw him at our school. We split up years ago. I am on my own now. And you?" "Also alone." Chris answered. "Perhaps we might call each other by our first names. I am Chris." "And you must call me Ursula" was the answer.

As the afternoon was pleasant they then decided to walk along the Thames Embankment, past Cleopatra's Needle and then The National Theatre walking along the avenue of trees and stopping to sit on the benches facing the river. Near Embankment station they found a café and ordered tea and cake. Afterwards they made their way back to Euston and boarded a train for the return journey. They sat beside each other. As the train was drawing into their destination Ursula turned to Chris and said "I have enjoyed today. We saw so much. And I enjoyed being with you." "The day is not over yet," said Chris, "Why don't we walk through the park and find a pub for a drink?" Ursula agreed to the suggestion and they walked through the park in the evening sun and sat down on a bench. "It's a pity that you are going back to Germany after the weekend" Chris said. Ursula smiled, looked at him and laid her head on his shoulder. Chris felt the warmth of her body as she snuggled up to him. He put his arm around her and then kissed her. Ursula responded to his kiss. They remained like this for some time and then got up and found a pub to have a drink. For the rest of the evening they talked about their lives, where they had grown up, been to school, studied and worked. Then Chris walked Ursula back to the house where she was staying. "Can we meet again tomorrow?" Chris asked. "Yes. After lunch", Ursula relied " I have only packing to do, but I don't want to go back now."

Chapter 6

Chris and Ursula met the following day in the afternoon. They embraced, kissed and then walked hand in hand to the park and the boating lake that was busy with parents and their children. Chris asked Ursula what her plans were for the summer holidays. "I would like to come back to England for a few weeks" was her reply. "Where will you stay?" Chris asked. Ursula replied, "Oh, I will look around for somewhere to rent. You see, I would really like to work here." Chris was surprised at this remark and he asked her "You mean that you would like to teach here?" to which Ursula answered "Well I could teach German in a secondary school." Chris then told her "Do you know that another school in this town is looking for a German teacher?" Ursula's eyes lit up. "I must call at this school tomorrow before we go back to Germany. It would be wonderful if I could work here " and with this remark she flung herself into Chris's arms and they embraced.

The next days before departure Ursula collected application forms from the school Chris had mentioned. They had not received any applicants as it was late in the school year and this was a good sign for any applicant for the post.

Chris and Ursula continued to spend time together for the last days of the exchange and on the last evening after a meal together in a restaurant they ended up at Chris's house. They were completely attracted to each other and very much in love. Later Chris walked Ursula back to her host's house and as he kissed her good night he said, "If you get this job, which I hope you do, you can come and live with me." "Thank you. I will" was her reply.

Some months later the neighbouring school to Chris had a German native speaker in the Languages Department and Chris was no longer on his own in the house.

The End

GROUP THERAPY

Chapter 1

Pete Taylor sat at his computer putting the finishing touches to what he had been writing over the last few days. It would soon be time for him to stop and go out visiting. Such was the accepted regular pattern of a Minister of Religion and probably had been so for centuries. The old adage or joke that "The vicar only works on Sundays" was nowadays modified by the perceived routine of "Mornings for study and sermon writing, afternoons for visits and evenings for meetings". However, recent decades had changed much of this. Most people were now at work during the day and so many visits had to be done in the evenings or at weekends. The social shift had affected all spheres of employment. There were, nevertheless, the elderly, the housebound and those ill in hospital where the preferred visiting hours were still afternoons. So Pete finished what he was writing, shut down the computer and looked at his list of people to visit after lunch.

Pete was single and this was his first church where he was in charge. He had been in this post about two years. Prior to his training for the ministry he had been in the Armed Forces as an officer in the Royal Air Force. He began as a junior officer and then progressed to being in charge of welfare of personnel. After a number of years he decided to leave the service and train for Christian ministry. This had come about through his attendance and involvement at a local church where he had discovered faith and had been active in the youth work. Feeling that he wanted to do more in the church he talked things over with the vicar and eventually was selected for training as a minister. He felt he had achieved his ambition and calling.

Pete ate a simple lunch of soup and bread, drank a cup of coffee and then set off on foot to make the three visits he had on his list. The first visit was to an elderly couple living in a terraced house in the centre of town. He spent an hour with them, listening to news of their children and families, hearing about visits to doctors and the ensuing tales of ailments. Then he moved on to make a visit to a gentleman who had recently been widowed and after his wife's funeral he had joined the congregation. His last visit of the afternoon was to a retired single lady called Ellen who had had a career in the Civil Service. As he partook of Ellen's tea and biscuits Ellen declared that she had asked Pete to visit her as she had some questions for him and was hoping that he would be able to answer them. Ellen's questions were concerning outreach. She asked Pete what the church was doing to reach out to those in the community who might have questions about religion. Pete replied that anyone was welcome to attend church services but this answer was in no way to Ellen's satisfaction. "But how are people to find a faith if they have no way to ask questions and receive answers?" she asked. "They could stop behind and ask me after the Sunday services" Pete answered. Ellen was quick to respond "Yes, but that would assume that they wanted to come to church anyway. Most people don't see the relevance of going to church but they still have questions about religion. About why we are here and what our purpose in life might be -where they are going afterwards- if there is an afterwards. Existential and spiritual questions." Pete thought for a moment and then asked "Have you yourself got any idea how the church might help people with this?" "Well, yes, I have" Ellen replied, "we could hold a series of meetings for people to come and ask questions and receive answers. A sort of open discussion. We could advertise a series of sessions with a list of topics for discussion, have someone like yourself introduce the topic for the session and then open the meeting for discussion, questions and answers. We would also provide refreshments. It's been done in other churches." Pete then asked Ellen to compile some facts for an agenda item at a church meeting, where and when to hold the sessions, how many volunteers would be needed and what sort of refreshments. Then he left the matter with Ellen and made his exit. This had been a visit that was much different from the norm and he went back home a little shaken and disturbed. He consoled himself with the fact that it had been Ellen's and not his idea and she would do the groundwork necessary.

Some weeks later at the church meeting Ellen's proposal came up on the agenda. Sadly it was not received with any degree of enthusiasm. After a brief number of questions to Ellen the parishioners asked Pete for his thoughts on the idea. Put on the spot, Pete did not give a convincing argument and so the item was shelved for the time being. In a way, Pete was relieved. Not so Ellen, who after the meeting expressed her bitter disappointment to him. Ellen requested that Pete look again at her idea and make preparation to represent it in the not too distant future. Pete said that he felt that without the enthusiasm of the majority of parishioners the idea was not going to become a reality and so he consigned the whole issue to the back of his mind.

Chapter 2

Some weeks later Pete was in the church hall visiting the parent and toddler group when one of the organisers came up to him and said that there were two people in the entrance lobby asking to see the vicar. Pete went out to the entrance and there was a couple, probably in their late thirties, ordinarily dressed and waiting for him to appear. "Hello. I'm Pete Taylor, the vicar. I was told that you wished to see me." The couple introduced themselves as Rob and Sarah and explained that they had recently been exploring religion and wanted to find out more about the Christian faith. Would the vicar be able to help? Pete was at first taken aback by this since most callers usually wanted to use the church building for some purpose and did not come for questions of faith. He thought for a moment, said he was involved with a group at the present and then asked Rob and Sarah to leave contact details and he would be in touch shortly. Rob and Sarah seemed satisfied with this reply and then they left. Pete realised that he had made excuses rather than see the couple now. He thought of his recent conversation with Ellen. She had been right. There were people out there in the community with questions. And so he decided to talk to Ellen once more.

Later that afternoon Pete called on Ellen who was very excited at what he told her about the couple calling at the church that morning. "Now will you set about arranging something?" she asked Pete. "Well, at the church meeting there wasn't much positive interest so what could we do?" he replied. Ellen said that they could work out a programme, venue, dates and times and put the details in the parish newsletter. If Pete was concerned about holding such an event on church premises because there had not been any definite congregational support then the meetings could take place in her own home. They agreed to meet later in the week and put something together.

Over the next week Pete and Ellen drew up a six weeks programme of meetings on a Friday evening to take place in Ellen's home. There would be refreshments on arrival and Pete would open the meeting with a short introduction to the week's topic, after which there would be time for discussion, questions and answers. The series would be open to all and they could accommodate a maximum of ten participants. The couple that had called to see Pete would be informed. After all, it was in part due to them that the event was being planned. In addition to the parish newsletter they would put some notices in local shops, the community centre and other public venues. Then it would be just a question of waiting to see if there was any interest.

Chapter 3

When the first Friday of the intended meetings came round, Ellen had prepared food and drinks. She had set out ten chairs in her large conservatory and when Pete arrived everything was ready. The meeting was planned for seven thirty p.m. All they needed now were guests. Would anyone turn up? Just before seven thirty the doorbell rang. The visitor was a woman in her thirties who gave her name as Pat. Then the bell rang again and this time it was a man of around fifty whose name was Joe. As they all were offered refreshments, made introductions and took their seats the doorbell rang once more. This time it was Rob and Sarah, the couple who had previously called at the church to see Pete. So the group for the first evening comprised four guests, a member of the congregation and the vicar.

After refreshments, Pete thanked everyone for coming and explained the format of the evenings. He would introduce the evening's topic and then it was up to everyone to ask questions and take part in conversation. The first topic was entitled "Why believe?" When Pete had finished his introduction there was at first a silence after which each of the guests asked questions. The idea was for everyone to discuss and for Pete to be responsible for answering specific questions relating to Christian faith and practice. The conversation went well and just before nine thirty Pete drew the meeting to a close. He thanked everyone for coming and said that he hoped to see everyone next week. Then the guests left. Pete stayed behind to help Ellen clear up and ask her how she thought the evening went. She was pleased. Then Pete left for home.

As a consequence of the meetings being advertised in the parish newsletter there were some members of the congregation who asked Pete how the first evening had been. What was more surprising was that an older couple, John and Val who had been part of the congregation for decades came up to Pete and asked him "Can anyone come to these meetings?" "Well, yes," Pete answered, "It's a way of reaching out to those outside in the community who may have questions about our faith." "But what about people in the congregation who may have questions. Can't they come?" Val asked him. "I never thought of that," Pete confessed. Val didn't leave the matter there and she followed up with the question "What if they missed the first meeting. Could they still turn up?" Now Pete was in the realm of things he had not thought of. He stalled and then said, "Of course they can." "Well," Val answered "In that case we will join your group next Friday." Then she and John left for home.

Chapter 4

On the Friday of the second meeting John and Val joined the others and so there was a total of eight persons in the group. Once again discussion was lively, questions having been put and answers explored. All this was quite new to Pete. His role as a vicar had largely consisted of leading church services, meetings and visiting parishioners. In the main, the only people he met who were not congregation were those who came to ask about events such as weddings and funerals or to hire the church hall. When their planned events had taken place these people vanished back into the community.

After the third Friday meeting Pete called on John and Val, the older couple belonging to the congregation, to ask how they had found the meetings. John and Val said that they had learnt things that they had never known about, in particular the fact that prayers didn't only have to be read out of a book at church, you could use your own words and pray anytime, especially when in need. This they had discovered at last Friday's meeting that had been entitled "What is prayer?" Pete was both encouraged and perturbed by this remark. Did it mean that there were others in the congregation who were similar in their knowledge and experience? It was the tendency to think that matters of faith were 'caught' and not 'taught', but here was evidence that some instruction might be necessary and possibly welcome.

The following Friday's meeting was about exploring the Bible. Joe, an older member in the group said that it seemed a long book and asked if one had to start reading at the beginning and then plough through to the end. Rob and Sarah, the couple that had originally come to see Pete wanted to know if the Bible gave instructions for living since they felt that they had made mistakes in their lives. Sarah, the single woman wanted to know what was said about life and death, and John and Val the two members of the congregation said they only really knew the stories about Jesus and didn't read books anyway.

All this gave Pete plenty to think about. He began to feel that he wasn't doing much good as a vicar. He told Ellen as much and her answer was "Well, what did you expect? This is what outreach is all about. Meeting people where they are. You've just come up against some of this, that's all. Be encouraged!"

Chapter 5

During the next week Rob and Sarah made an appointment to come and see Pete. He received their visit at the church at their request. They sat down in one of the rows of seats in one of the side aisles. Rob opened the discussion by saying that both he and Sarah had been married before to other partners and they had met each other some time after their respective divorces. They were not married and had been living together for two years and now Sarah was pregnant. "We would like to get married in church. For us it would be a sign of a new start. Would this be possible?" Rob asked. Pete's brain was attempting to compute all the details and work out an answer and so he said "We'll talk about it when our Friday meetings have finished. I promise." "Thank you," Val said, "We'll look forward to that."

On the following Sunday after the church service Pete had three unexpected conversations in the porch as he was saying goodbye to the congregation. John and Val came up to him and asked if he might be able to teach them how to read the Bible. Then, almost the last person to leave was Joe, who had also been coming to the Friday meetings. "I thought I'd come on a Sunday to see what it was like" he said to Pete. "And what was it like?" Pete answered. "Better that I expected. No need to wear a suit and much more informal. Thank you. See you Friday."

On the next Friday everyone was at the meeting with the exception of Pat. The evening went well and the group decided to bring some party food for the final session in a week's time. As Pat had not been present, Pete looked up her contact details and sent a message. By the end of the weekend there had been no response and so he phoned. No reply. He left it another day and then decided to call at her address in the evening when he supposed she might be home from work. This he did. He arrived at the house and rang the doorbell. No answer. He waited and then rang again. Nothing. He was just about to walk away when the door opened and there was Pat. She did not look well and had obviously been crying. "Are you alright?' Pete asked. "Not really" was her answer. "Can I be of any help?" Pete ventured to ask. Pat said nothing at first and then she replied, " No...wait...can you come in for a minute?" so Pete followed her inside. Pat led the way to the sitting room and asked him to take a seat.

There was a long silence, after which Pat began to speak. "I found out last Friday morning that my brother Dave had been killed in a car crash. I was at work and I just had to leave everything and go. I only got back home yesterday." Pete asked about Pat's family. "My parents were older than most and they both died some years ago. Dave was my only brother. Now only I am left." Pete was at a loss to say anything sensible. Eventually he found some words "Is there anything I can do, or help you with?" Pat was silent for a while and then said, "The funeral will be a cremation service. Will you take the service for me? I feel I need someone who knows me to do it. I don't want it to be a stranger." Pete agreed to this request. The crash had taken place near Dave's home, which was about three hours drive away. He could easily make time to conduct the service. He told Pat to give the funeral director his contact details and he would liaise with the funeral director and Pat. Pete also wondered about leaving Pat alone with her grief. He could not offer her a room to stay in the vicarage but he did think of Ellen's house. "I don't believe that you should be here alone at the moment. At least till after the funeral. I could phone Ellen and ask if you could stay with her for a while." Pat at first resisted the suggestion but then she saw the sense in it. "Please do. If it's not too much trouble." So Pete arranged it with Ellen and Pat went to Ellen's.

On the following Friday it was the final session in Ellen's home. Pete asked the members of the group what they thought of the time that they had spent together over the six weeks. The general consensus was that it had lived up to expectations and they all wanted a series of follow on meetings. A break of a fortnight was agreed upon and then there would be another four sessions.

Chapter 6

It was during the recess that Pete arranged the cremation service for Pat's brother Dave. Pat came to the vicarage several times and together they worked out an order of service. Pat asked Pete to read out the eulogy she had prepared as she thought that she would not be up to reading it out on the day.

The day of the funeral came. Pat travelled up with Pete in his car. The funeral was scheduled for two o'clock in the afternoon so they found a café to have a coffee beforehand. Then they drove on to the crematorium.

The service took the usual twenty minutes. There were some of Dave's friends present and some of his work colleagues. Pat sat alone at the front of the chapel, facing Pete as he conducted the service from the lectern. When the service was over people stayed for a while to talk to Pat and then they all left. "I suppose we should drive back now," Pete said as they made their way to his car in the car park. "Shall we stop somewhere on the way back and have a meal? We haven't had any time to eat so far." "Yes, that would be good" Pat replied.

After driving for a couple of hours they stopped at a roadside pub and went in. They decided to have a full meal as a welcome distraction from the other business of the day.

As they began the meal Pat said to Pete "Thank you for coming with me today and thank you for taking Dave's service. I'm glad it was you. I wouldn't have wanted anyone else to do it." "I was pleased to do it. It was a privilege. I am glad that we got to know each other on the evenings at Ellen's home"' Pete answered. "Perhaps we could continue to meet each other?" Pat asked. Pete thought he had guessed what Pat was trying to express and so he answered, "I'd like that. What would you suggest?" "We could go out somewhere each week. I'm on my own, now with no family and you're on your own. It might be good for us both. What do you think?" Pete thought many things but he agreed to Pat's suggestion. He had never thought that one couple calling at the church a couple of months ago might begin to effect a change in so many people's lives. Of the group that had met as a consequence of one couple's enquiry, Ellen had used her home for hospitality, Joe had started going to church, John and Val had found answers to longstanding questions, Rob and Sarah wanted to marry and start a family and now it seemed as if he and Pat might not be alone in the future.

The End